THE DEAD BOYFRIEND

Also by R. L. Stine

SERIES

Goosebumps

Fear Street

Mostly Ghostly

The Nightmare Room

Rotten School

INDIVIDUAL TITLES

It's the First Day of School . . . Forever!

A Midsummer Night's Scream

Young Scrooge

Red Rain

Eye Candy

The Sitter

R. L. STINE

THE DEAD BOYFRIEND

A *FEAR STREET* NOVEL

THOMAS DUNNE BOOKS
ST. MARTIN'S GRIFFIN
NEW YORK

THOMAS DUNNE BOOKS.
An imprint of St. Martin's Press.

THE DEAD BOYFRIEND. Copyright © 2016 by Parachute Publishing, LLC. All rights reserved. Printed in the United States of America. For information, address St. Martin's Press, 175 Fifth Avenue, New York, N.Y. 10010.

www.thomasdunnebooks.com
www.stmartins.com

The Library of Congress Cataloging-in-Publication Data is available upon request.

ISBN 978-1-250-05895-9 (hardcover)
ISBN 978-1-250-11199-9 (international, sold outside the U.S., subject to rights availability)
ISBN 978-1-250-09206-9 (e-book)

Our books may be purchased in bulk for promotional, educational, or business use. Please contact your local bookseller or the Macmillan Corporate and Premium Sales Department at 1-800-221-7945, extension 5442, or by e-mail at MacmillanSpecialMarkets@macmillan.com.

First U.S. Edition: September 2016
First International Edition: September 2016

10 9 8 7 6 5 4 3 2 1

For Blade

Many Happy Returns

PART ONE

1.

*H*ere I am, my dear diary, about to confide in you again. About to spill my guts, as I always do, only to you. This is the only place I can open my heart and talk about what I really feel. How many ballpoint pens have helped me share my story with you? How many late nights have I nodded off, my head drooping over your opened pages, my hand still clenching the pen, as if I could write my thoughts in my sleep?

Of course, my parents don't understand why I spend so much time bent over my desk, scratching away line after line, baring my soul when I could be doing a million things for fun. But you do, my friend. *Sigh*—

Okay. Shall we start today with some details? Since this is a new diary, I'm going to begin at the beginning. I'm Caitlyn Donnelly. I'm seventeen, a senior at Shadyside High. I'm not terrible looking. I'd say I'm a seven.

I have nice wavy blondish hair that falls nicely down my shoulders. I'm average height and weight. I have an okay smile although my two front teeth stick out a little. My friend Julie says my eyes are my best feature because they're so round and dark and serious.

I've lived in the same house on Bank Street, two blocks from the Shadyside Mall, my whole life. It's just my parents and me. Jennifer, my older sister, moved to LA to be a screenwriter.

Jen is the talented one in the family, but so far, she spends most of her time waiting tables at a taco joint in Westwood. I think I spend more time writing than she does, but I know she'll get a break one of these days. She's very sophisticated and clever, and everything comes so easy to her.

Jen and I were never that close, I guess because she's almost six years older than me. But she was someone I could talk to when I had things on my mind. Like, always. And I miss her a lot.

We FaceTime every few weeks, but it isn't the same. It's always kind of awkward, I think because Jen feels she's been out in LA for nearly a year and hasn't come close to getting anyone interested in her writing. And she's the kind of person who hates to fail.

I don't care if anyone ever sees my writing, Diary. Truth is, I don't want anyone to *ever* see it. I think I'd totally freak if someone read my true thoughts and learned what a weirdo I am. That's why I keep the book locked and wear the key on a chain around my neck.

Private. Keep Out. This Means You.

Actually, I don't think I'm a weirdo. I just don't fit in with my family. They're all so driven and ambitious and serious about life, and I mainly want to have fun. *Sigh* again.

Life is so short. I've learned that the hard way. You know all about it, Diary. You're the only one.

No one else knows the true story. No one would believe it.

Since Blade died, my life is only sadness. And fear.

I don't think I'll ever get back to the cheerful, funny, fun-loving person I was. My parents and my friends are desperate to pull me from my black mood.

But how can they? It will never happen.

Blade and I were perfect together. Perfect . . . from that first night we met.

That night . . . It wasn't a perfect night, Diary. I ran into Deena Fear that night.

I'd lived in Shadyside my whole life and never spoken to anyone from the Fear family. And now my hand is suddenly sweaty and it's hard to grip the pen, remembering . . . thinking about Deena Fear and all the darkness she brought with her.

And poor Blade. My beautiful Blade. Did I have any way of knowing he would be with me for such a short time? Any way of knowing he would die such a horrifying death?

I have to stop. My tears are smearing the page. And I'm gripping the pen so—tightly now. I want to use it to stab . . . stab . . . stab. . . .

2.

It seems like a long time ago, but it was only a few weeks, Diary. Julie and Miranda and I were squeezed into a booth at the back of Lefty's. That's the cheeseburger place across from the high school. The food at Lefty's isn't bad, but we mainly go to see who else is there. It's a hangout. That's what they'd call it in all those cornball teen movies.

It was a little after nine on a Friday night. Just about every booth was filled with kids from our high school. A few grumpy-looking adults were huddled by the front counter waiting for a table. They probably didn't appreciate the loud voices and constant laughter.

I think adults generally hate teenagers. Because they're jealous. They'd rather be teenagers than what they are.

A loud crash made us all jump. A waitress had dropped a tray of glasses. The restaurant went silent for a few seconds. Then everyone burst into applause.

I turned back to Julie and Miranda. "What was I talking about?"

"You were talking about yourself, of course," Miranda said. She's the sly one with the dry sense of humor.

"Well, it *is* my favorite subject," I replied.

"You were telling us about the little boy who dropped his popcorn," Julie said.

"Oh. Right. Well, I'm not allowed to replace it. Ricky, the manager, says no free popcorn for anyone. But I waited till Ricky stepped away from the popcorn counter, and I gave the kid another bag."

"Big whoop," Miranda said. "That's your best story for tonight?"

I grabbed her wrist. "You didn't let me finish," I said. "Then the kid dropped the second bag, too."

Julie laughed. "That's so sad."

Miranda rolled her eyes. "Caitlyn, you have an exciting life. My heart is totally pounding. Tell that story again."

"Okay, okay," I said. "So, working the popcorn counter at the Cineplex isn't a thrill a minute. What did *you* do today that was so exciting?"

Miranda sighed. "Believe it or not, this cheeseburger is the highlight of my day." She raised it to her mouth and took a small bite. The tomato slid from the bun and plopped onto her plate.

"You have to learn how to work a cheeseburger," Julie said. It wasn't that funny, but all three of us laughed.

Julie and I have been friends since ninth grade, although we're both very different. She's always sarcastic and rolling her eyes and making funny remarks. I'd say her sense of humor is kind of nasty, actually.

I'm not a rah-rah cheerleader, but I try to see the bright side of things. I get into things. I'm enthusiastic. I can't help it. I don't hold myself back. I even try to enjoy things other people might find boring, like my after-school shifts at the popcorn counter.

I'm impulsive. And emotional. I cry at movies and TV shows all the time. It doesn't embarrass me.

I don't think I've ever seen Miranda cry. Or get very excited about anything, either. She's always standing off to the side, making jokes. She's not shy. She's just all locked-up inside herself, I think.

Miranda could be really attractive if she lost a little weight and did something with her stringy brown hair. Also, her glasses have to go. The red plastic frames make them look like swim goggles.

Julie and I keep telling her she'll look so much better with contacts. But she says she doesn't want to stick sharp little things in her eyes. Stubborn.

I'm not judging her in any way, Diary. I'm just trying to describe her. She's a good friend. She'll never see what I write here. No one will. But I want to be as accurate and honest as I can.

Julie doesn't eat meat, so she had a grilled cheese sandwich, and we shared a plate of fries. She and I look like we could be sisters. Her hair is pretty much the same blonde as mine, and we both have serious, dark eyes. She likes to wear bright red lipstick, which makes her face more dramatic than mine.

We're the same age, but I think she looks older. Maybe because she's about two inches taller than I am. And, I admit it, she dresses better. Her aunt is always sending her these awesome designer tops and skirts from New York.

Julie is very practical and even-tempered. Her last name is Nello, and I call her Mellow Nello. She's always warning me not to jump into things and to be careful about different guys and to take it easy and not be so emotional.

I always accuse her of being too timid and not taking chances, of always being predictable. Of course, she thinks being predictable is a *good* quality. We may look alike, but our personalities are way different.

Miranda leaned close and gave my hair a long sniff.

I squinted at her. "Are you getting weird?"

"No. Your hair smells like popcorn," she said. "It's a great smell. Someone should make a popcorn perfume."

"A million-dollar idea," Julie said. "I'd buy it. And how about bacon perfume? We could make a fortune."

"I thought you were a vegetarian," I said.

She frowned at me. "I don't eat bacon. That doesn't mean I can't *wear* it."

I sighed. "When I get home, I shampoo my hair twice. But I can't get rid of the popcorn smell."

Julie shook more salt onto the plate of fries. "Do you ever eat any of the popcorn while you're waiting for the next customer?"

I grinned. "Ricky would like to keep count of each kernel, but he can't. I help myself to a handful or two when he isn't looking."

Miranda rolled her eyes again. "Are we going to talk about popcorn all night? Doesn't anyone have any good gossip?"

I gave her a gentle push. "Get up. I have to go to the bathroom."

She edged out of the booth and climbed to her feet. I slid out behind her. "Don't say anything interesting till I get back."

"Not a problem," Miranda said.

Lefty's has a single bathroom across from the kitchen door. I had to wait in line behind two other girls I knew from school. They were talking about a metal band concert they'd seen at the Arena in Martinsville. They thought it was awesome. They sat in the third row, and the ushers passed out ear plugs to keep everyone from going deaf.

Then the girls started talking about what the warm spring weather was doing to their hair. "Extra conditioner," was one solution. "I use half a bottle of the stuff every morning." Interesting idea.

When I came out of the bathroom, I walked right into a girl with long straight black hair, dark eyes, and black lipstick against pale skin. She was carrying a white take-out bag of cheeseburgers.

The bag slipped from her hand when I bumped her. We both bent over to pick it up, and we cracked heads.

"Sorry," she said quickly, in a tiny voice. "Sorry." Even though it was my fault.

I handed her the bag.

I knew who she was.

Deena Fear.

I didn't know that my life was about to change forever.

3.

Deena Fear wore huge round black-framed eyeglasses. Her dark eyes appeared to bulge behind them, making her look like an owl. She wore a long-sleeved black crew-neck sweater, despite the warm night, over a short straight black skirt and black tights. I noticed her earrings—small silver skulls. She had a silver skull in her nose, too.

"I'm sorry," I said awkwardly. "I wasn't watching where I was going. I—"

"That's okay, Caitlyn." I felt a quick jolt of surprise. I didn't think Deena knew my name. Her eyes went down to my wrist. "I like your bracelet." She gazed at the silver bracelet my parents had brought me from their vacation in the Bahamas.

To my surprise, she reached out and wrapped her hand around my wrist and the bracelet. Her hand was warm and dry. Her fingernails were divided down the middle, each one half-black, half-white. She held my wrist for a long moment. "Does it have powers?"

She spoke in such a soft voice, I wasn't sure I'd heard correctly. "Powers? The bracelet?"

She nodded. Her straight black hair fell over her forehead. She let go of my wrist to brush it back.

"I . . . don't think so," I said. I laughed. Was she making a joke?

She shifted the cheeseburger bag to her other hand. "I've seen you at the mall, Caitlyn," she said.

I nodded. "Yeah. I work at the Cineplex some afternoons." I turned and glimpsed Julie and Miranda watching from the back of the restaurant. "I'd better get back to my friends. See you around, Deena."

Her owl eyes locked on mine. I wanted to turn away, but they seemed to hold me there. "Sometimes I see things," she said. "Sometimes I know things about people."

I didn't know how to reply to that. A waitress carrying a tray of cheeseburgers over her head wanted to squeeze past us. I used it as an excuse to get away. I gave Deena a little wave and walked away. For some reason, my wrist felt all tingly where she had handled my bracelet.

Miranda climbed up so I could slide into the booth. I sat down in time to see Deena Fear walk out of the restaurant, her long hair sweeping behind her back.

"Since when do you know her?" Julie asked.

"I don't," I said. "I almost knocked her over. So we started talking."

"She takes Goth to a new level," Miranda said.

"She gives me the deep creeps," Julie said.

"She isn't so bad," I said.

Miranda shook her head. "Just because she's in the Fear family, does she have to wear all black clothes and have black lips and black nails and creep around like some kind of witch? Why doesn't she rebel? Wear hot colors? Be a cheerleader? Run for Prom Queen?"

Julie laughed.

"She seems really shy," I said. "She's so awkward. Think she has any friends? Ever see her hanging out with anyone at school?"

"I don't remember even *seeing* her in school," Julie said.

"She doesn't *try* to have friends," Miranda insisted. "We were at the same birthday party once. I tried talking to her. But she's obsessed with ghosts and the paranormal and the walking dead. She kept talking about these movies I never heard of. At least, I *think* they were movies."

"Maybe she doesn't have a choice," I said, not exactly sure why I was defending Deena Fear. I guess I always like to side with the underdog. Or maybe I just like to argue with Miranda. "Coming from that family—"

"She's like a total Fear Family cliché," Julie chimed in.

My bracelet still tingled, as if it had been electrified somehow. I ate a few fries. They were cold now. I turned to Miranda. "Are you having a graduation party?"

She didn't hear me. She was staring at a table near the front of the restaurant.

"Miranda has to have the party," Julie said. "I can't have it. My house is too small."

"We could have it in your backyard," I said. "My parents aren't even going to be in town. They'll be in South Africa for two weeks on a business trip. Do you believe they're missing graduation?"

"Then we should have the party at *your* house," Julie said. "No parents. A total blowout."

Miranda still had her gaze on the table at the front. She bumped my shoulder. "Who's that guy gawking at you over there? Do you know him?"

I followed her gaze. A blue-uniformed waitress began to clear a table, blocking my view. "What guy?"

"See him?" Miranda turned my head. "The guy in the red hoodie? He's been staring at you like he's hypnotized."

"Hypnotized by your beauty," Julie said. I couldn't tell if she was making a joke.

I finally spotted the guy, by himself at a small, square table, sitting sideways in his chair, ignoring his food. And yes, his eyes were on me. He was kind of cute looking. A dark shirt under the open, red hoodie. A wave of black hair falling over his forehead. "I don't recognize him," I said.

"He thinks he knows *you*," Miranda said.

I squinted harder. "No. I've never seen him. I don't think he goes to Shadyside."

"He hasn't blinked," Julie said. "Maybe he wants to have a staring contest with you."

"I'll find out," I said. "I'm not shy." I gave Miranda's chubby arm a shove. She obediently climbed to her feet so I could slide out.

Julie raised her hand to her mouth. She does that a lot. She's so easily shocked. "Are you really going over to him?"

"What's the big deal?" I muttered. I squeezed past two girls who were just sitting down at the table across from us, and I strolled over to Mr. Red Hoodie.

He had amazing gray-green eyes, and they grew wider as I stepped up to him. I placed my hands on my waist. "Hey," I said. "How's it going?"

He shrugged. "Not bad." He had a nice smile and a tiny crease of a dimple in one cheek.

"Were you looking at me?" I demanded.

He snickered. "Do you always think people are looking at you?"

"Answer the question," I said. "Were you?"

He shrugged again. "Maybe." I liked the way those incredible gray-green eyes crinkled up when he smiled.

I smiled back. "Why were you looking at me?"

"Because you have a piece of lettuce stuck on your chin." He reached up, tugged it off, and showed it to me.

Well, yes, Diary, I was expecting something a little more romantic. Of course, I was embarrassed. But I didn't want to turn and hurry away. Something about him—not just his cuteness—drew me to him.

I crossed my arms over my chest. "What's your name?"

"Blade."

"No. Really," I said.

"Really. It's Blade. My parents wanted me to be sharp."

I laughed. "Bet you said that line before."

"It's the truth," he said.

"My name is—" I started. But he raised a hand to cut me off.

"Let me guess," he said. "I'm good at guessing names. I have a talent."

I slid past him, pulled out a chair, and sat down across from him. I glimpsed Julie and Miranda in our booth in the back. They were both watching the scene intently. "Shoot," I said.

His eyes burned into mine. He studied me. "Your name is Tabitha," he said.

I nearly choked. "Tabitha?"

He nodded. "What do your friends call you? Tabby?"

I nodded. "Yes. They call me Tabby. How did you guess my name like that? That's amazing. Did somebody tell it to you?"

His cheeks turned pink. "No way. I told you. I have a talent for guessing names."

I leaned across the table and flashed him a teasing look. "And what else do you have a talent for, Blade?"

He shrugged. "What's your real name?"

"It's Caitlyn."

"I thought so. That was my second guess."

A few minutes later, after some definite first-class flirting, I said goodbye to my two friends and walked out of the restaurant with him. Where were we going? I had no idea. I only knew that after just a few minutes, I felt totally comfortable with him. More than comfortable. I was definitely attracted to him, and I wanted to spend time with him.

Is this what love at first sight is all about?

Hard to believe, but the question actually flashed through my mind as we stepped out into a warm April night, a soft, cool breeze brushing my hot cheeks, the fragrant aroma of Lefty's cheeseburgers in the air, a bright half-moon overhead in a purple sky.

I know, I know. It sounds like some kind of bad Lifetime movie. But sometimes life has to imitate that strange unreal happiness you usually see only on TV.

And this was definitely one of those times.

Blade put his hand on my back as we walked. It seemed totally natural. As if we'd been walking together for years. I found myself wondering if he felt the same way.

We strolled along Division Street, past the high school, the yellow moonlight reflected in its dark windows, and along the houses that stood across from Shadyside Park.

What did we talk about? I hardly remember, Diary. We talked about school. Blade's family moved to Shadyside last fall, and he goes to The Academy. That's the private high school across town. He talked about his old house in Shaker Heights and how he hated to leave his friends back there.

He said he plays keyboard and guitar, and he is in a jazz quartet at school. He's pretty sure he can get into Oberlin. But he was sick for a semester, so he can't graduate with the rest of his class in June.

I told him I was accepted at Middlebury College in Vermont, which is where my sister Jen went. But my parents hadn't been able to work out a student loan for me yet. I said I'd tried for a Creative Writing Scholarship, but the competition was too stiff. I didn't get it.

He turned those awesome gray-green eyes on me. "You like to write?"

I was about to answer when something across the street caught my attention. I heard blaring dance music and saw the bright lights in a large house across the street. Through the front window, I could see a crowd of dancing people. The crowd spilled out onto the broad front porch. Voices and laughter.

And I had one of my ideas. I grabbed Blade's arm. "Hey, Blade," I said. "Let's do something crazy.

4.

*H*e narrowed his eyes at me. "How crazy?"

"Let's crash the party," I said. "You know. Hang out. Dance for a bit. Get something to drink." I motioned to the front window. "Look. It's so crowded. No one will notice two more people."

I held my breath, waiting for his answer. This was definitely a test. Would Blade pass it?

A grin spread over his face. "Love it," he said. He grabbed my hand and started to pull me across the street. "Let's *do* this thing. Party time."

That's when I knew Blade and I belonged together.

We raced up the front lawn. Two beds of tulips stood on either side of the front porch. A soft wind made the tulips bob and sway as if greeting us. We made our way past the people on the porch, nodding and saying hi, acting as if we belonged.

They seemed to be college age, maybe in their early twenties. They were casually dressed, not quite as casually as Blade and me. But we didn't really stand out. They were drinking wine from paper cups, talking in small groups, glancing at their phones as they talked.

We slipped through the screen door and stepped into the living room. It was hot in there, so many bodies jammed in. Electronic dance music was cranked up to full volume. The room buzzed and vibrated to the beat.

The lights were turned low. It took a while for my eyes to adjust. Blade held my hand and we crossed the room to the drinks table. Three or four couples were dancing. But the room was too crowded, and they kept bumping people clustered on the sides.

Blade and I grabbed bottles of beer. I don't really like beer. I guess I was trying to impress Blade. On the next table, I saw big bowls of tortilla chips and salsa and a tray of pigs in blankets.

I turned and gazed around the room, squinting into the shadowy orange light. I didn't recognize anyone. They were all definitely older than Blade and me.

I pressed my face close to Blade's ear. "I wonder whose party this is."

He gazed around. "Beats me."

We clicked beer bottles. "This is very cool," I said.

"Best party ever!" Blade joked.

A young woman with very short blonde hair, shaved on one side, and pale blue eyes, dressed in faded jeans and layers of blue and green T-shirts, bumped me, nearly spilling her wine. "Oh. Sorry," she said. "No room to move."

"No problem," I said. "Awesome party."

She nodded. "I've never seen you here before. How do you know Hannah and Marty?"

"Just from around the neighborhood," I said.

She moved on. Blade and I enjoyed a good laugh.

And that's when I saw her. Deena Fear. My breath caught in my throat. She was so unexpected, so out-of-place.

Deena sat at the bottom of the stairway that led upstairs. Dressed in black as always, she had her pale hands clasped tightly in the lap of her skirt. Her black hair fell loosely around her face.

I peered at her through the railings in the banister. Did she see me?

Yes. Her eyes flashed behind her owlish glasses. She jumped to her feet.

I nudged Blade with my elbow. "That girl who's coming over—"

Blade squinted through the crowd as Deena approached. "Do you know her? Is she a friend of yours?"

"No," I said. "I mean—"

Deena stepped through a dancing couple to get to us. Her face was even paler than usual, and her lips were covered in a neon purple lipstick. She stepped up to me, a few inches too close. I mean, she didn't give me any space at all.

"Hi, Caitlyn."

I nodded. "Hey, Deena."

She swept her long hair behind her shoulders with one hand. "Caitlyn, do you know Blade?"

"Well . . ." I hesitated. How did she know Blade's name? He didn't go to our school.

I glanced at Blade. He was studying her intently, like she was another species or something.

"How's it going, Blade?" Deena asked.

"Not bad," he said. He squinted at her. "Do I know you?"

She didn't answer him. Instead, she startled me by grabbing my wrist, wrapping her fingers around my silver bracelet, just as she had at Lefty's. I felt a shock of warmth travel up my arm.

"Great party, huh?" Her eyes peered into mine, as if searching for something. I tried to free my arm, but she held on.

She squeezed my wrist, so hard the silver bracelet cut into my skin. Then she brought her face close to mine. I felt her hot breath on my cheek.

"I saw him first," she whispered.

5.

blinked, my mind suddenly whirring. I knew I hadn't heard correctly. The music . . . the voices . . . It all seemed to grow louder, as if I was swimming in sound. Drowning . . .

I didn't say anything. I guess I was too stunned to react. And, I just wanted to free my arm from her grip, to get away from her.

"We should get going," Blade said, his eyes on the front door.

I tried to turn, but Deena held on. She raised my hand close to her face, puckered her bright purple lips, and blew on the silver bracelet. Blew a puff of hot breath onto the bracelet and my wrist.

Her breath felt damp, almost sticky, on my wrist. I gasped and tugged my arm free. The bracelet tingled, then grew burning hot. "Hey, Deena—" I called out.

But she had already spun away from us. She bumped a few startled people out of her way and disappeared out the door, her long tangles of black hair swaying behind her.

I held my wrist, waiting for it the bracelet to cool.

Blade's face was twisted in confusion. "What was *that* about?"

"Dunno," I murmured. "Seriously. I don't have a clue."

"She is weird with a capital weird," he said.

"Her name is Deena Fear," I told him, stepping out of the way of a young man carrying a large pizza box to the food table. "She is a Fear. Do you know about the Fear family?"

He shrugged. "Not really."

"I'll tell you about them sometime. They're famous here in Shadyside." I stepped back to avoid another pizza box coming through. "Do you want to leave?"

He grinned at me. "So soon? I think our hosts would be hurt if we left this early." He put a hand on my shoulder and guided me toward the food table. "I'm hungry. I didn't get to finish my cheeseburger, thanks to you."

Blade folded a slice of pizza in his hand and started to eat it hungrily. We talked to a couple across the food table. The woman was studying to be a vet. The guy said he was working on a blog and a YouTube channel. They asked us if we knew a place to go sky-diving in Shadyside.

That's kind of a laugh, if you know Shadyside.

I caught a tall red-haired woman watching Blade and me from the kitchen door. She had a puzzled expression on her face, like she was trying to place us. I wondered if she was Hannah, one of the hosts.

The front door swung open and several more couples arrived. The red-haired woman hurried to greet them. There was a lot of hugging and cheek kissing.

Suddenly, I had another idea.

Did I want to show Blade how crazy and bold I could be? Did I want to see if he was as impulsive and crazy as me? Maybe.

He was pulling a string of pizza cheese off his fingers. I tugged him close. "Blade, I have another idea. How about this? It could be a riot," I said. "How about we stand in the middle of the living room and start kissing? You know, like we're really into it. We're all over each other. Kissing like we should get a room somewhere."

He nodded. His eyes flashed. "That could work."

"It would be a way of thanking our hosts," I said, grinning. "You know. Give them a little entertainment."

He pulled me into the center of the room. "Caitlyn, I like the way you think."

He wrapped his arms around me and pulled me to him. He was stronger than I'd imagined. He held me so tight, I struggled to breathe.

And then he lowered his face to mine, and we began kissing. A long kiss. It made me even more breathless. I wrapped my hands in his hair, then lowered them to his back. We both had our eyes wide open, watching each other, enjoying the joke. Enjoying the kiss . . . Enjoying . . .

I glimpsed people moving out of our way. Couples stopped dancing, their faces twisted in surprise.

Blade and I ground our lips against one another's, being as showy as we could. I soon realized it wasn't just a joke, not just a way to shock people. We were kissing each other for real, with real feeling.

When did the joke end and the true emotion kick in? I don't know. I only know there wasn't enough time to enjoy it. Because the pounding dance music cut off suddenly. A hush fell over the room. And then I saw the red-haired woman striding toward Blade and me, her face tight with anger.

"Who are you?" she called. "Do I know you? Who brought you here?"

Blade and I clung to each other for a few seconds more. Then we broke apart and watched her approach, her hands balled into tight fists at her sides.

"Who are you? Do you belong here?"

"Oops," I said. "Sorry." I couldn't think of anything better to say. But then I added, "Awesome party." Then Blade and I took off, barging through some startled guests. Out the front door. It slammed behind us.

We ran down the driveway, laughing, shrieking, stumbling. As giddy as I'd ever been in my life. Was it the greatest night of my life? Probably.

We held hands and ran full speed till we reached the corner. No one was coming after us. I stopped and hugged a streetlight to catch my breath.

Blade was bent over, holding his knees, gasping for breath. "Awesome party. Awesome party." He repeated my farewell line. He shook his head. "I can't believe you said that. That was classic."

"Ow." I felt a stab of pain at my wrist and realized my silver bracelet still felt hot. I backed away from the streetlight and raised my arm to the light.

"What's wrong?" Blade straightened up and walked over to me.

"It's my bracelet," I said. "This is so weird. It's burning me."

"Well, take it off," he said.

I moved the fingers of my other hand to the clasp. I'd never had any trouble snapping the bracelet off. But now I was having trouble finding the clasp.

I smoothed my thumb and pointer finger around it. The bracelet seemed solid. A solid band of metal. "This is impossible," I murmured. "I . . . I can't find the clasp."

Blade took my arm. "Let me try." He held my arm high, lowered his face, and eyed the bracelet closely.

"Turn it over," I said. "Spin it so the clasp is on top."

He tried to turn the bracelet. "Ow!" I cried out again. He tried to spin it in the other direction. Pain shot through my hand and up my arm.

Blade let go of the bracelet. He raised his eyes to me. "Caitlyn, the bracelet won't slide. I think . . . I think it's melted onto your skin."

6.

"**N**o, Julie. The jeweler couldn't get it off. He said he didn't have the right kind of saw for silver."

I had the phone to my ear in one hand and pushed the shopping cart with my other. Whoa. I stopped just in time. I almost rear-ended a woman with a little girl riding in her cart.

"Well, what are you going to do?" Julie asked. "You can't just leave the bracelet on forever. It'll cut off all your circulation!"

"Do you think?" I said sarcastically. "Think I haven't thought of that?" I turned the cart into the produce aisle. Blade was ahead of me, halfway toward the frozen foods section. "My dad says he's going to talk to a surgeon. You know. Like a bone surgeon. Someone who can cut off the bracelet without taking my hand off with it."

"I-I . . . don't believe it," Julie stammered. "And you really think Deena Fear—"

"I don't know what to think," I said. "It's not like she

has super powers. Something happened to the silver. I don't know what. Something made it melt, I guess." I sighed. "At least it cooled down. It isn't burning hot anymore."

"Weird," Julie said.

I grabbed a head of iceberg lettuce with my free hand and dropped it into the shopping cart. "I've got to go," I said. "I'm at the Pay-Rite. With Blade."

"Excuse me? Caitlyn, you're food shopping with Blade? Are you moving in together or something?"

"Ha-ha. Very funny. I'm shopping for my parents. Blade came along because—"

"Caitlyn, here's some unwanted advice from me," Julie said, lowering her voice. "Maybe you're going too fast with Blade. Maybe you should be more careful. You know. Take it slower."

"You're right," I said. "That *was* unwanted advice. I'll talk to you later, Julie." I clicked off and tucked the phone into my bag.

Blade held up a gigantic frozen pepperoni pizza. "Is this on the list?"

"No. Maybe on *your* list, but not my parents'. Go put it back."

He turned and walked back down the aisle, twirling the pizza box on one finger. I checked the shopping list again. My parents were making some kind of stew to take over to my cousin in Martinsville.

"Celery . . ." I pushed the cart alongside the produce shelves. An old Beatles song played in the background. In

the next aisle, a little boy was crying his eyes out, screaming because his mom wouldn't let him have a cookie.

Blade got there before I did. He grabbed a thick bunch
of celery and tore off two sticks. He tossed a stick to me.
"*En garde!*" he shouted. He came at me waving his celery
stick, slapping it against mine.

I turned away from the cart and began to duel. Our celery swordfight became intense. I get aggressive with a stick
of celery in my hand. Slapping at his stick, I drove Blade
back. His arms flew up as he tumbled into a cereal box
display, and the boxes went toppling noisily onto the floor.

I heard a few gasps. People were watching us with stern,
disapproving faces. I saw a red-faced young man in a long
white apron hurrying toward us, waving angrily.

Blade and I tossed our celery sticks into the cart. I
brushed my hair back, took a deep breath, and prepared
to face the angry store worker.

"What's going on here?" he demanded breathlessly,
lowering his hands to the sides of his apron. His name tag
read: CHUCK W. He had short brown hair spiked up in
front. His face was very red. I could see beads of sweat
on his forehead.

"We . . . had an accident," I said, motioning to the cereal boxes strewn across the aisle.

"Yeah. An accident," Blade repeated. We both put on
our most sincere faces. "We're sorry."

"They just fell," I said. "Can we help you pick them
up?"

He glared angrily at Blade, then me. "An accident?" He lowered his gaze to the celery sticks in the shopping cart. He stared at them a long while. He seemed to be thinking hard, considering how to handle this.

Finally, he sighed and shook his head and said, "I'll take care of it. Have a nice day." He walked off, wiping his sweaty forehead and muttering something about "teenagers."

A few minutes later, Blade and I were lifting the groceries into the trunk of my mom's Toyota. "Where did you learn those moves with a celery stick?" Blade asked.

"I took lessons after school," I said. "I wanted to be a celery fighter in the Olympics. But my parents couldn't afford the grocery bills."

He kissed me. "You sure you have to go to work?"

I nodded. "It's my duty. I don't want to deprive people of their popcorn."

We had fallen into a warm and teasing relationship. We felt so good together in such a short time. I kissed Blade again, said goodbye to him, and drove home to drop off the groceries.

On the way, I thought of Julie's warning. *Slow down with Blade.* I knew she meant well. She wasn't being jealous or mean. She's known me forever, and she knows I can go overboard sometimes.

I'm an emotional person. As I said, I cry at movies. Maybe I hug people a little too long. Maybe I get hurt more easily than some people. One cross word from someone makes me feel like I'm a total failure.

That's me. You can't help being who you are, Diary. And why not live life *large*. I mean just grab the bull by its horns. Go whole hog. Live everything to the fullest.

Well . . . listen to me go on and on. I've become a real philosopher ever since I met Blade. Ever since I fell in love with him. Face it, Caitlyn. You're in love with him. It was love at first sight.

And maybe that was making me a little crazy. A little hyper. A little more *bonkers* than I was before.

Later that night, maybe I overreacted to what happened. After my shift behind the popcorn counter . . . the most frightening minutes of my life . . . Maybe I overreacted. But that's just me. What can I do?

7.

I was daydreaming about Blade, Diary, my elbows on the popcorn counter, gazing at the nearly empty movie theater lobby. Someone had spilled a plate of cheese nachos on the floor in front of the men's restroom, and Ricky, the manager, was mopping up the mess. He was in a bad mood. But what else is new?

The popcorn machine was nearly full. It was a really slow night. I thought about helping myself to a bag of Twizzlers. I hadn't had any dinner. But with Ricky in such a foul mood, I decided it wasn't a good idea.

Ricky is twenty-four or twenty-five. He's lanky and blond with freckles around his nose and cheeks. He has these big hands that look like cartoon hands because they're too big for his skinny arms. Everything about him is bony and awkward. His jeans are too big, and the Polo shirts he wears are droopy and wrinkled.

He's almost always in a grouchy mood. I think it's because he doesn't want to be the manager here. He told me once he planned to go to Penn and be a Business major. But he didn't get accepted and now he takes courses online, and he still lives at home with his mother.

My phone vibrated. I pulled it from my pocket. A text from Blade: *C U tomorrow?*

Ricky finished mopping and walked over toward me, carrying the mop and bucket. I slid the phone back into my jeans. "Caitlyn, don't just stand there," he said.

"There's no one here," I said, motioning with one hand. "What am I supposed to do?"

"Wipe off the display case counters," he said. "Check the ice machine."

I nodded. "No problem." I'd learned not to argue with him. I wanted to keep this job. It was pretty easy, and it paid fifteen dollars an hour (and all the popcorn I could sneak).

I found a cloth in back and started to wipe down the glass countertop. My stomach growled. Those Twizzlers looked mighty tempting. I was at the far end of the counter when I saw someone enter the lobby.

It took me a few seconds to recognize Deena Fear. I stared at her as she approached the counter. She wore a dark purple sweater over a short black skirt and black tights. Her purple lips matched the sweater.

Her long black hair flowed down her back in thick tangles. She had dark mascara circling her eyes. It made me think of a raccoon.

Is she following me? Why am I suddenly seeing her everywhere?
The questions made my whole body tense up. I could feel my muscles tighten. "Hey, Deena." I tried to look casual.

She leaned her hands on the counter, her black fingernails glistening, smearing the glass I had just wiped. "I remembered you work here," she said.

I nodded. "What movie are you seeing?"

She pointed to Auditorium Four. "*Vampire High School III,*" she said.

I should have known.

"The first two were awesome," she said. "Life-changing. Seriously."

"I . . . didn't see them," I said.

"I love the books, too. I have them all. It's the *best* series."

Over her shoulder, I saw Ricky watching us from the doorway to Auditorium Two.

"How's Blade?" Deena asked. The raccoon eyes peered into mine.

"Fine," I said. Ricky didn't like for us to chat with people. We were supposed to stick to business. "Do you want some popcorn or something?"

She ignored my question. Her fingernails tapped the countertop. "Sometimes I see things," she said, lowering her voice to a whisper. "Good things and bad things."

I felt a chill. I suddenly remembered my bracelet. How

her hand wrapped around it. How it burned hot, then melted onto my skin. I lowered my arm, keeping the bracelet out of sight.

"I . . . don't understand," I said.

"I want you to be my friend," she whispered, not lowering her gaze, not blinking. "I don't want anything bad to happen to you."

"Uh . . . thanks," I murmured.

Ricky hadn't moved. He was still watching, an unhappy look on his face.

"Does Blade talk about me?" Deena asked.

My breath caught in my throat. "Talk about you? Well . . ."

"Does he? Does he talk about me?"

"Well . . . I don't know," I said. "About what exactly?"

Her eyes still hadn't blinked. She kept them locked on me. The tiny silver skull on the side of her nose appeared to gleam. "We should talk," she said finally. "We could be friends, right? We could be friends and sit down together and talk about Blade?"

I was too stunned to hide my surprise. "Talk about him? You mean?"

Her expression changed. Her eyes went dead. "I see," she murmured. Her pale hands clasped together over the countertop. "I see. You don't want to talk. I get it."

"No—wait," I said.

She slammed her hands on the glass. Behind me, the

popcorn machine suddenly started to crackle, making new popcorn. I jumped at the sound.

I turned to the machine in surprise. Beside it, both soda dispensers began pouring out soda. Sparks flew from the glass hotdog warmer. It buzzed and shorted out.

"Hey!" I shouted.

Across the lobby, I saw the alarm on Ricky's face. He came trotting toward us, shouting my name.

Deena had a triumphant grin on her purple lips. Her dark eyes flashed. "Sure you don't want to talk?"

I lunged to the back counter to shut off the soda dispensers. The soda was already puddling on the floor. My sneakers sank into the sticky, dark liquid.

I saw Deena slide her hands off the glass countertop. She edged back a step.

Popcorn began flowing over the sides of the machine like lava pouring out of a volcano. I struggled with the soda dispenser. The levers were stuck. A river of soda ran behind the counter.

"I know we'll talk," Deena said. And then she whispered, "Sorry about your bracelet."

Over the rattle of the popping popcorn and the rush of the soda pouring onto the floor, I wasn't sure I heard her right. "What did you say?"

But she turned and began to stride quickly toward Auditorium Four.

Ricky stepped breathlessly to the counter. "What's

happening? What's happening here? Why did you turn everything on?"

"I didn't!" I cried. "I didn't touch anything."

Ricky swung himself over the counter. His shoes splashed in the soda on the floor. He reached behind the dispensers and pulled the plugs. I hit the *Stop* button on the popcorn machine again and again. Finally, it slowed and the crackling and popping stopped.

Ricky and I both stood there, breathing hard, staring at the incredible mess.

"This is impossible," I muttered, shaking my head. "This can't be happening." I turned to Ricky. "I didn't touch anything. I swear. I was talking to the girl from school and . . . and . . ."

Ricky swept a bony hand back over his hair. "Must have been a power surge," he said. "Some kind of power problem. From the electric company. That's the only thing that could have caused this."

"Yes," I agreed. "A power surge."

But I didn't believe it. I believed it was a warning from Deena Fear.

Ricky walked to the supply closet to get mops. I pulled a large trash can behind the counter and began shoving the extra popcorn into it.

I had no idea the evening was going to get even worse.

8.

The soles of my sneakers were sticky from the spilled soda. My shoes made swamp noises—*thwuck thwuck thwuck*—on the concrete of the mall parking lot as I made my way to my car.

It took Ricky and me nearly an hour to clean up the counter area. We worked in silence, but every few minutes Ricky muttered, "How could this happen?"

I had a pretty good idea. But of course I couldn't share it with anyone. Who would believe it? If I said Deena Fear had power over those machines, people would lock me up as a crazed psycho, and I wouldn't blame them.

I now realized that she had a thing about Blade. I probably should have caught on earlier. But what did that mean? Did she plan to ruin my life with wild stunts like with my bracelet and the movie food machines? Was that her plan to win Blade?

That didn't make any sense at all.

I pictured her dark-circled eyes burning into mine, as

if trying to penetrate, to invade my brain. And again, I heard the creepy *click* of her long black-and-white fingernails on the counter glass.

My head was swimming with these crazy, impossible thoughts. I debated whether or not to tell Blade about Deena, about how she kept asking about him, asking if he ever talked about her.

Did he know her before I met him? He said he didn't. I should believe what he told me. He said he'd never heard of the Fear family.

Blade hadn't lived in Shadyside for long, but that was a little hard to believe. I think when people move here, they are told immediately to steer clear of the Fears and Fear Street.

I always thought it was all superstition and made-up stories about them. But with Deena around, I was no longer so sure.

With all these thoughts making my brain whir, I walked past my car. I stopped and tried to remember where I'd parked. Level C. And the sign in front of me told me I had walked all the way to D.

Get a grip, Caitlyn.

I turned and started to walk back, my sticky shoes *thwacking* on the concrete. I guess the sound kept me from hearing the footsteps behind me.

I didn't realize I was being followed until the man was only a few feet behind me. I heard the rapid scrape of shoes and wheezing breath.

I didn't have a chance to run. I didn't even have a chance to be scared. Until he grabbed me roughly and spun me around to face him.

I stared into the red eyes of a thick-stubbled face, angry, half-hidden behind the hood of a dark hoodie. I'd never seen him before.

He squeezed my shoulders and shook me hard, the red eyes glowing, his jaw clenched.

"Let me go!" I screamed. My voice rang loudly off the concrete parking garage walls. I whipped my head around. "Help me! Somebody!"

But the hooded man and I were alone.

"Give me your wallet. I can hurt you." His voice was a harsh rasp from deep in his throat. He squeezed my arms so hard, pain shot up and down my whole body.

I struggled to breathe. "Let go," I choked out in a frantic whisper. "Let me go. Please . . ."

9.

He was wheezing now, spit rolling over his lips.
"I can hurt you," he repeated. "Your wallet. Hurry."

I forced myself to breathe. My heart was thudding so hard, my chest ached. "Okay," I choked out.

Still holding my arms, he lowered his head, brought it close to mine, so close I could smell his sour breath.

I knew this was my chance, Diary.

I'm not the kind of girl to give in easily, to surrender without a fight. I knew this was the moment those self-defense classes I took last year would be useful.

I arched back a few inches, as if trying to pull away from him. Then I brought my right leg up. I snapped it up hard and fast. He uttered a startled gurgling sound as my knee smashed the middle of his face.

I heard a sick *crack*. The sound of his nose breaking.

His hands slid off my arms. He grabbed his face, as bright red blood began to spurt from his nose. With an animal howl of pain, he dropped to his knees. He covered his face with both hands. Blood flowed through his fingers, down the front of his hoodie. He howled again.

I stood there for a long moment, gasping for breath, enjoying my victory, my heart thudding in my chest . . . thudding so hard I could feel every throb of blood.

I watched him for a second or two. Then I forced my legs to move. I took off, my sneakers pounding the concrete, ran to my car, and drove away.

"Wow. Is it heavy? Can I hold it?" Julie asked.

"The handle is pretty awesome," Miranda said. "How do you open it?"

"This button here," I said, raising it to her face. "You press it with your thumb and the blade slides open." I waved it around. "It's a stainless steel blade. Careful. It's amazingly sharp. It'll cut through anything."

We were in the small den at Julie's house, and I was showing them the knife I had bought at Hunters & Company, at the mall, the knife I planned to carry in my bag from now on.

The guy at Hunters told me all about it and how to use it. It's called a Magnum Ypsilon Tan G-10 Folding Knife. The handle is black-and-tan and it feels great, heavy but not too heavy, comfortable in your hand. The blade is amazing.

I told the salesman my dad was a collector, and I was buying it for a birthday surprise. I think he believed me.

I don't think he could see on my face that I was buying it for protection, buying it for me.

"This is dangerous," Julie said, shaking her head. "I know you went through a bad thing, Caitlyn, but . . ."

"It's just for emergencies," I said. "I'm not going to walk around stabbing people."

"You're not allowed to bring it to school," Miranda said. "If you get caught . . ."

"I won't get caught," I said. "You know that big bag I always carry. I'll keep the knife at the bottom, under everything else."

They tried to argue. But they know me. Once I make up my mind, that's it. I knew I'd never use the knife. But having it with me made me feel better.

I got lucky in the parking garage with my knee kick. But what if that creep had come after me? What if he had tried to kill me?

The thought made me shudder. I still thought about it all the time, still pictured his stubbly, drooling, red-eyed face, still felt his hands squeezing my arms.

My phone beeped. I tucked the knife into my bag and pulled out the phone. "A text from Blade," I told them. "We're going out tonight." I tapped a reply. "We text each other all day long. It's awesome."

Julie and Miranda exchanged a glance. I knew what was coming. Their lecture on not getting too serious about Blade.

Well . . . it was too late for that. I couldn't be more

serious, and I knew he felt the same way, too. But for some reason, my friends thought it their duty to caution me.

"You always rush into things, Caitlyn."

"You're always so impulsive. You don't really know Blade that well. You really should be careful not to get carried away."

I rolled my eyes. "I seriously am beginning to believe that you two are jealous," I said. "I'm sorry you don't have boyfriends, but it really isn't my fault."

Julie jumped to her feet. "That's not fair. We're only thinking of you," she said.

Miranda motioned for her to sit back down. "Okay, okay, we get it, Caitlyn. You don't want us in your face. Fine. We'll stop."

Julie sighed and dropped back down.

"Blade and I are perfect," I told them. "I know we haven't known each other for long. I know it's all been so crazy and fast. But . . . we're perfect. I don't know how else to say it."

They both sank back into the couch cushions. I think I finally got through to them.

A short while later, I went home to get ready for my date with Blade. For a long while, I sat on the edge of my bed, daydreaming about him. I imagined his arms around me, holding me tightly against him. I pictured those strange gray-green eyes gazing so deeply into mine. I thought about the way we teased each other, the way we talked together so easily.

I thought about kissing him . . . kissing him till I felt lost . . . till I felt I was somewhere else in the world . . . somewhere far away from anyone and anything I knew.

When my phone beeped, it shocked me from my dazed imaginings. I grabbed my bag and fumbled the phone out.

I read the short text message on the screen—and gasped, "Oh no."

10.

The message from Blade was short: "Can't make it tonight. Got hung up."

I read it over and over, as if I could get the words to tell me more. Why didn't he explain what the problem was? Why didn't he at least say he was sorry?

He must have some emergency, I told myself. He must be as disappointed as I am.

I punched his number into the phone and raised it to my ear. My hand was trembling. I knew I was overreacting, but I was very disappointed. My daydreams had gotten me all psyched to see him.

The call went right to voicemail. I listened to his voice: "This is Blade. You know what to do." I didn't leave a message. I knew I'd talk to him later. I knew he'd explain everything. And maybe we could get together later tonight.

Dinner with my parents seemed to last forever. I hadn't told them much about Blade. I usually blurt out everything about my life to them. I'm not the kind of person who can hold anything in. But for some reason, I'd decided to keep Blade to myself.

My parents are totally great people. They're not always in my face and pretty much treat me as an adult. They put up with my enthusiasms and my wild mood swings and my general insanity. And they're not always trying to pry into my life.

I think they'd love to know what's in my diary. But trust me, that's totally off-limits to them. As I said, I keep it locked and I wear the key on a chain around my neck.

My dad is big and healthy-looking. I guess you'd call him robust. He brags that he still has all his hair at forty-three. Mom teases him that that's his biggest accomplishment.

She likes to deflate him whenever he gets too full of himself. She says it's her hobby.

He works out at a gym three days a week, and he's a cyclist. He gets up at six most mornings and rides his racing bike for ten miles along River Road to the top.

He's an administrator at Shadyside General Hospital. He says he just shuffles papers all day and deals with hospital staff problems. That's why he likes to get a lot of exercise and fresh air before work.

Mom could be really hot-looking if she paid attention to her looks. But she isn't really interested in what she wears or her hairstyle or anything. She wears a lot of baggy T-shirts and these dreadful Mom jeans.

She mostly has her blonde hair tied back in a tight ponytail, and she refuses to wear any makeup. She says she likes the fresh look. But just a little blusher and some color on her lips would make her look five years younger.

She teaches Business Ethics at the junior college in Martinsville. And she gives lectures at companies on the subject. I don't really understand what she talks about, but she reads three newspapers a day online and every book on business that comes out.

So there we were at dinner. When it's just the three of us, we eat in the little breakfast nook beside the kitchen. It's a snug little area, lots of sunshine through the windows, and a picnic table and benches where we eat most of our meals. The dining room is saved for company, so we use it mostly on holidays.

Dad had brought home take-out fried chicken and mashed potatoes with gravy. Usually my favorite, but I didn't have much appetite tonight. You know why, Diary.

I stared at the leg and thigh on my plate. Mom was talking about some kind of lawsuit against a company I'd never heard of and why it should be thrown out of court. Dad tsk-tsked and spooned more mashed potatoes onto his plate.

"Do you have a date with that boy tonight?" Mom's question stirred me from my thoughts.

"Uh . . . not tonight," I said. "I think I'm just going over to Miranda's and watch some videos or something."

Mom leaned across the table toward me. "What's his name again?"

"Blade," I said. "Blade Hampton."

"Funny name," Mom muttered. "No one has normal names these days. Do you know anyone named Jack or Joe or Bill?"

I laughed. "No. No, I don't."

"You've gone out with this guy a few times," Dad chimed in. "Why don't you invite him over sometime?"

I was pretty much keeping Blade to myself. Not exactly keeping him a secret, but not eager to share him with my parents. "Yeah. Okay," I said. Always better to agree and not start a controversy.

Dad changed the subject to how he pulled a muscle racing his bike this morning and how his leg had stiffened up. One of my parents' best qualities is that they have very short attention spans. They can never stay on a subject for more than a minute or two.

I gnawed on the chicken leg for a while and forced myself to eat some of the potatoes and coleslaw. Mainly so Mom and Dad wouldn't start asking more questions. I couldn't stop thinking about Blade. Wondering what was up with him.

After dinner, I changed into a long-sleeved top. The weather had turned cool and the sky was heavy with rainclouds. I called goodnight to my parents and hurried out to the car.

A few raindrops dotted the windshield as I drove to Miranda's house. She lives on Heather Court in North Hills, the ritzy neighborhood of Shadyside. Her house is big, with a zillion rooms, but very comfortable. Her parents collect very large old movie posters, so there are these great stars like Charlie Chaplin and Humphrey Bogart staring out at you from every wall.

Miranda is into old movies, too. If Julie and I are hanging out at Miranda's house, we usually end up watching some old black-and-white flick from the forties or fifties on Netflix. I love seeing the weird old clothes—everyone wearing hats all the time, even indoors—and the funny cars.

The rain was just a drizzle but I started the wipers. They squeaked as they scraped over the windshield. I turned onto Mission, which curved around to Miranda's street. I slowed down. There were a lot of cars on Mission. Drivers use it as a shortcut to River Road.

I pulled through a stop sign—and then let out a soft cry. "Whoa."

Was that Blade's car up ahead? I squinted through the rain-spotted glass.

Yes. It had to be.

Actually, it was his dad's car, but he drove it a lot. A '95 red Mustang. Not too many of those on the road in Shadyside. Leaning over the wheel, I read the license plate. Yes. Yes. Blade's car.

I lowered my foot on the brake. I didn't want him to see me. I didn't want to get too close.

But . . . who was that in the car beside him?

Bright white headlights beamed from an oncoming

truck swept over Blade's car and lit it up as if setting it on fire.

And I saw her. A girl. Beside Blade. A girl with short white-blonde hair. I just saw the back of her head. I didn't see her face.

His car pulled away from a stoplight and roared forward.

My hands squeezed the wheel. They were suddenly clammy and cold.

I lowered my foot to the gas. I knew what I had to do. I had to follow them.

11.

My headlights washed over the back of the red Mustang. I slowed down, let more space separate our cars. I had a sudden urge to tromp on the gas and plow right into him. Send that blonde girl flying through the windshield.

A crazy thought, and I quickly suppressed it. What kind of person would imagine such a violent, evil thing?

The girl beside Blade had to be a cousin. Or a family member who needed a ride. Or a friend from his old school he hadn't seen in months. Or . . . Or . . .

Weird how your brain can dance around when you're upset or anxious.

The rain stopped. I shut down the scraping windshield wipers. The red Mustang made the turn onto River Road. A few seconds later, I turned, too.

The road curves along the bank of the Conononka River, a long, winding road that climbs into the hills over Shadyside. It was too dark to see the river. But I slid my passenger window down so I could hear the gentle lapping of the water against the muddy shore.

I thought the sound might calm me. But, of course, it didn't.

Again, my headlights played over the back of the Mustang. I slowed and edged to the right and let another car move between us. I didn't want Blade to see me. I didn't want him to think that I was suspicious, that I didn't trust him.

He was obviously dealing with an emergency. That's why he didn't have time to explain to me what was going on.

But . . . if it was an emergency, why was he turning into the parking lot at Fire? Fire is a dance club on River Road. It's a club for adults, but a lot of Shadyside students go there because the doorman isn't very careful about checking your ID. If you don't look twelve, you're in.

A neon sign at the street has red-and-yellow flames dancing into the air. A sign beside it reads: SHADYSIDE'S PREMIER DANCE CLUB. LADIES FREE.

The club was a long, low, red building with red and blue lights along the flat roof. A red carpet led to the awning over the entrance. The doorman stood behind a narrow wooden podium at the front of the awning. Even with the car windows closed, I could hear the drumming beat of the throbbing dance music from inside the club.

As I watched the red Mustang roll over the brightly lit gravel parking lot, a wave of nausea rolled over me. I was supposed to be with Blade tonight. He told me he got "hung up." So why was he here at a dance club with that blonde girl?

My ideas about a family emergency were quickly exploding, vanishing into air. And I fought down my dinner, which was rising to my throat. Fought down a choking feeling as I saw him pull into a parking place at the side of the club and cut his headlights.

My car rolled slowly over the gravel as I hung back, leaning over the wheel and squinting into the glare of the red, blue, and yellow lights overhead. I stopped and backed into a space between two SUVs near the club entrance.

When I looked back, Blade and the girl were out of his car. Blade wore his red hoodie over slim-leg jeans. She was tall and thin, taller than him, and the lights played over her pale face and the short white-blonde hair.

She leaned into Blade, and he slid an arm around her shoulders. They staggered sideways together, laughing.

A sob escaped my throat. I forced myself to breathe.

I told him I loved him. That night in his car up on River Ridge, the stars above us, the sparkling river down below, when we held each other, held each other as if we were the only two people on earth. We kissed . . . we kissed and . . . and . . .

I grabbed the door handle, ready to jump out of the car. I had an impulse to jump out, run across the gravel lot, grab him, grab him and spin him around, and—

—*No.*

I squeezed the steering wheel, squeezed it until my

hands ached—and watched them kiss. She turned to him and he wrapped his hands around her neck and pulled her face close. And they kissed again. The red-and-blue lights played over them, making it look like a carnival scene or some kind of glaring dream.

If only.

If only it wasn't real, Diary. But it was happening, and I was there.

I shoved open the car door. It slammed into the SUV next to me. I didn't care. I slid out and stumbled forward, away from the car. I couldn't balance. The world tilted and swayed under me.

My whole body shuddered as I forced myself forward.

Did I cut the engine? Switch off the headlights? I don't remember, Diary.

Blade and the girl stopped at the doorman's podium. He was a wide hulk of a guy, shaved head, wearing a purple sleeveless T-shirt that showed off his tight biceps and tattoos, and baggy gray sweatpants. Blade pulled something from his wallet—probably a fake ID—and the doorman waved them into the club.

"Stop!" I opened my mouth in a cry, but no sound came out. I took a deep breath. My shock quickly turned to anger.

Blade is a liar! A liar and a rat!

I couldn't erase the picture of them kissing from my mind.

Suddenly, I knew I had to confront him. I had to let him know that I was here and I saw him.

A cry of rage burst from my throat. Like an angry animal. And I roared forward, my sneakers kicking up gravel, ran full speed toward the club entrance, the red-and-blue lights flashing in my eyes, running blind, blind with my anger and hurt pushing me forward.

I had to get in there. I had to make him face me.

I was a few feet from the doorman's podium when a dark figure ran out from the side of the club. At first, I thought it was a moving shadow. It took a few seconds to realize it was someone dressed all in black.

Deena Fear.

I nearly ran right into her. She caught me with both hands before we collided. I was panting, wheezing loudly, enraged.

"Deena—what are you doing here?" I choked out, the words rasping against my dry throat.

"He betrayed us!" she cried. "Caitlyn—he betrayed us!"

12.

I gaped at her. The red-and-blue lights reflected in her glasses made her eyes look on fire.

"He betrayed us!" she screamed again, gripping my arms tightly.

"Go away!" I cried. Blade was inside the club with the blonde girl. I didn't have time for Deena Fear. I had to keep my anger burning. Or else I'd never be able to confront him.

"Get off me!" I swung my body hard and tugged free of her grip. Then I lowered my shoulder and shoved her out of my way, shoved her so hard she toppled backward over the gravel. Her glasses flew off her face and landed on the ground.

I spun away, lowered my head, and ran past the doorman. I heard him shout: "Hey—stop!" And then he uttered a string of curses as I pulled the door open and rushed inside.

Into the flashing lights and throbbing beats, deafening,

almost painful. I could see the silhouettes of dancers in the middle of the floor. Couples huddled around the sides. A crowd at the brightly lit bar against the far wall.

I took a deep shuddering breath. Then another. My eyes gazed from one wall to the other, squinting to see faces, to see Blade. The pounding beats matched my heartbeats. I stood there, gasping in the thick, humid air, inhaling the tangy aroma of alcohol and sweat.

I was so angry, so hurt, so devastated, the whole scene became a crazy blur to me. The lights pulsed with the beats of the music, pulsed with my heartbeats, until . . . until I was not myself. I was out of myself. Out of my head.

Where is he? Where?

And then my eyes stopped at the white lights of the bar. And I saw him. I saw Blade at the bar. The blonde girl was beside him. He was leaning over a tall barstool, talking to a female bartender.

I didn't hesitate. I lowered my shoulder and bolted across the dance floor like a running back. Couples dodged out of my way. I heard angry shouts:

"Look out!"

"Hey—what's your problem?"

My problem was Blade.

I let out a furious screech as I stepped up behind him. I grabbed his shoulders and spun him around.

His eyes opened wide in surprise. "Caitlyn?"

The words spilled from my throat. "What are you doing here?"

He regained his composure quickly. "Getting two beers," he said. He gave a casual shrug.

"Who *is* she?" the blonde girl asked.

"She's nobody, Vanessa," Blade said. "A friend. From school."

I felt as if I'd been cut in half, sliced right down the middle.

I stood there trembling with my mouth open.

I know I overreacted. I know I went ballistic. Totally lost it. But that's the way I am. That's me, and there's nothing I can do about it.

I am 90 percent emotion. And when Blade said those words to the girl, something inside me snapped.

"But . . . but . . ." I sputtered. "But we *love* each other!" The words tumbled out of my mouth before I could stop them.

Blade's face went entirely blank. His eyes appeared to freeze over. "In your dreams, maybe."

And there I stood, my world collapsing in a sea of flashing lights and dancing couples and pounding music.

Suddenly, Vanessa, the blonde-haired girl, moved toward me. She put a hand gently on my shoulder. "Are you okay? You're trembling. Can I get you a drink or something?"

Her dark blue eyes peered into mine. She was genuinely worried about me.

I stared back at her, unable to answer. Finally, I spun away and took off. I ran back through the dance floor, pushing my way through the dancers, startled cries all around me.

I pulled open the door and burst back into the cool darkness. The voices and music were a roar behind me. My eyes still pulsed from the crazy lights.

The doorman turned from his podium as I ran past him. "Hey, you—stop! Come here!" he bellowed angrily.

Again, I ignored him, my shoes slipping and sliding on the gravel as I turned toward my car. No sign of Deena Fear. I had a fleeting thought that she'd be there by the door waiting for me, waiting to grab me and insist that Blade had betrayed her, too.

Which one of us is crazy?

I knew the answer. I was the crazy one for caring too much. Everything I did in that club was crazy. So crazy that even the girl with Blade, a total stranger, was worried about me.

But I didn't care. Blade was so important to me. I trusted him. I believed in him. I loved him. And now . . . I didn't care. I didn't care. I didn't care.

He acted as if I was nothing. "She's nobody." That's what he told that girl Vanessa. "She's nobody."

And he was right. Now I was nobody. I thought I had something great, something wonderful to get through life. But now I was nobody.

I climbed into the car. Slammed the door. Started it up and roared out of the parking lot, sending up a tidal wave of gravel behind me.

Where was I going? I didn't know. I swung the car out of the parking lot without looking. To my left, a small van screeched to a halt. Close call. I didn't care.

I slammed my foot down on the gas pedal. The car lurched forward. The pull of speed felt good to me. I spun around the curves of River Road, sliding from one lane to the other.

I made the car squeal and scrape. The river flowed beside me. All I had to do was swing the wheel to the left, and I'd be over the side and into the water. The cold, fresh water. Was it a good night for a swim?

No. I slid the wheel to the right and followed the dark road. Was that a squirrel I almost hit? No. Maybe a rabbit. Maybe a raccoon.

I was making the big curve onto Parkview, doing at least eighty, when the oncoming headlights filled my windshield. I blinked in the blinding lights. I cursed them for having their brights on.

And too late, I realized I was in the wrong lane. I was in the left lane. Too late. Too late to swing the car. Too late to avoid them. I heard the roar of a horn, like a siren, as the lights grew even brighter, washed over me, blinded me.

I'm driving right into them. Can't stop.

13.

Sudden darkness. The long wail of the car horn ring-ing in my ears, bleating like an enraged animal. The horn finally stopped as the other car swerved into the right lane and roared past me.

Missed. The car missed. I forced myself to breathe. Silence now. The twin circles of bright white headlights lingered in my eyes.

Breathe, Caitlyn. Breathe.

Chill after chill ran down my back. A close call. I almost died. I didn't really want to die. I was too angry to die.

I jerked the wheel and pulled the car to the curb. I hit the brake too hard, and the car lurched forward before it stopped, throwing me against the wheel, then slamming me back.

I cut off the engine. Then I sat there with my hands in my lap, staring out into the darkness, forcing my breath-ing to return to normal.

Caitlyn, you're not handling this well. Caitlyn, get a grip.

Where was I?

I squinted across a narrow lawn to a square brick house with a single light on over the front stoop. A small one-car garage at the top of the driveway had its door open.

It took me a few seconds to realize I had parked in front of Blade's house. I stared at the yellow light over the stoop until the house blurred behind it.

I knew I didn't deliberately drive here. At least, I didn't *know* I was going to park in front of his house. "I should go home," I murmured out loud.

I reached for the button to start the engine. But then I lowered my hand to my lap. I needed to talk to him. No. I didn't want to see him. I didn't want to sit here for hours, till the middle of the night, waiting for him to return from his date. And then rush him, run at him, confront him crying and screaming.

No. I didn't want that.

So . . . why couldn't I start the car? Why couldn't I move? Why was I sitting here, every muscle in my body tense, my stomach rumbling and growling, wave after wave of nausea making me hold my breath and clench my jaw?

I don't know how much time passed. I glanced at the car clock when the red Mustang finally turned into the driveway. It was nearly one o'clock.

I watched the car stop in front of the garage. I watched the red taillights die. I watched the driver's door swing open. Now it all seemed to be in slow motion, like some kind of slowed-down dream.

Blade stretched his arms over his head. Then he closed the car door quietly. Quietly so he wouldn't wake his parents, I guessed.

I sat and watched, hands clasped tightly in my lap. When he started loping toward the kitchen door, I finally moved. I moved fast.

I shoved open the car door, grabbed my bag, and leaped out. I didn't bother to close it. I ran around the trunk to the driveway and began to run, gripping my bag in one hand, waving my other hand above me head. "Blade! Blade!" I shouted his name in a shrill voice I didn't recognize.

It was a warm April night, almost balmy, but the air felt cool against my burning cheeks. "Blade! Stop! Blade!"

Why did I drag my bag with me? I can't answer that question. Was I thinking clearly? Not at all.

Blade turned and I saw the surprise on his face. I kept waving my hand above my head as I ran, some kind of desperate signal.

I stopped a few feet in front of him, breathing hard, my chest heaving up and down.

He narrowed his eyes at me. "Caitlyn? What are you doing here?" No warmth in his voice. His eyes cold. Wary.

"I-I-I" I stammered. I searched for something good in

his face, just a tiny sign that he was glad to see me. No. Not even that. A sign that he *liked* me? No.

"It's late," he said, tugging the sleeves of his hoodie.

"I . . . I . . . Didn't you say you loved me?" I blurted out, my voice trembling as if underwater.

He blinked. He lowered his gaze to the ground. "We had fun," he murmured.

"Fun?" I cried. "Fun? You said you loved me. You know you did."

He raised his eyes. His mouth formed a sneer. "You didn't really think I was serious—did you?"

"Huh?" My mouth dropped open. I kept my eyes locked on him. I was straining to see the Blade I knew, the Blade I loved.

"We had fun, that's all," he said. He yawned.

I think it was the yawn that set me off. The loud, open-mouthed yawn put me over the edge.

I felt something in my brain snap. At that moment, at that second, something inside me cracked apart. I guess it was my whole life.

I really can't describe it. Something in my brain just exploded.

I saw the surprise on Blade's face. Or was it fear?

And then everything went crazy.

14.

"Fun?" I screamed. "Fun?"

He glanced to a window at the side of the house. His parents' room? Was he afraid I might wake his parents? Is that all he cared about?

"You *creep*!" I cried. I had the handle of my bag gripped tightly in my right hand. I raised my arm and swung the bag at him, swung it with all my strength.

"Hey!" Blade uttered a startled cry and stepped back. He lowered his shoulder, and the bag swung over his head.

"Hey, stop, Caitlyn. Stop it."

"Fun?" I shrieked. "Fun?"

I swung the heavy bag again. This time it glanced off his shoulder.

"Whoa." His expression turned angry. "I'm warning you," he murmured. "Stay back. Stop it."

My next swing caught him on the chest. I couldn't stop myself. I swung again, narrowly missing his head. I swung the bag again. Doubled him over with a blow to the stomach.

"Enough!" he groaned. He made a grab for the bag. Caught it from the bottom.

"Noooo!" I struggled to pull it away from him.

"Caitlyn—chill! Stop! Calm down! Can we talk?" He gripped the bottom of my bag and jerked his hands hard.

"Give it back!" I screamed. "Give it!"

The handle snapped out of my hand. I stumbled back. Blade held onto the bottom as we both watched all the contents spill onto the ground.

"You creep! You creep!" I was shrieking without even hearing myself.

Blade tossed the bag across the driveway. He glared furiously at me. "You crazy idiot. Are you going to leave?"

In the dim light from the stoop, I saw the knife. It lay on top of a scarf I had stuffed into the bag. With a shuddering moan, I dove for it. I gripped the handle tightly and raised it in front of me.

"Hey—what's that?" Blade demanded, gazing from the knife to me.

My thumb fumbled for the button, and I released the blade. It snapped out instantly and I held it in front of me so Blade could see it clearly.

"Come on, Caitlyn. Put that down," he said, holding his arms out at his sides, as if preparing to defend himself.

"Fun? We had *fun*?" I cried.

No way he could defend himself. I lunged forward and poked the sharp tip of the blade into the front of his hoodie.

He gasped and stumbled back. "Put it away. Are you crazy? Put it away!"

I jabbed at him, just enough to make him feel it. I poked him in the chest. Then I lowered the blade and poked his stomach.

"You're crazy! You're crazy! Stop. Put it down. Let's talk."

His eyes were wide. I could see he was in a panic. He kept his arms lowered, tensed, ready to fight back. He retreated a step, then another—and backed into his car.

I had him trapped now. I moved forward and poked him again, pushing the tip of the blade against his belly.

"Give that to me!" He uttered an angry scream and swiped at the knife.

I tried to swing the blade out of his reach. But instead, I sliced through the palm of his hand. The blade cut silently. I gasped. I started to choke.

Eyes bulging in disbelief, he raised his hand in front of his face as a line of blood oozed onto the palm.

The blood trickled for a few moments. Then it started to spurt.

We both stared at the bleeding hand in silence. It was too horrifying for either of us to make a sound.

And then he began to wail, shrill high-pitched cries, waving the spurting blood in the air.

Like a fountain, I thought. *Blood spurting like a bright fountain.*

His shrieks made my ears ring. The sight of the blood made my stomach lurch. I gagged.

I had to stop that horrible sound he was making.

I swung the knife back, then plunged the blade deep into his stomach.

Again. I stabbed him again. Stabbed again.

That stopped the screaming. He made a gurgling sound and grabbed his belly with both hands. Dark blood seeped through the red hoodie and poured over his hands.

He dropped to his knees, moaning, making strange wheezing sounds. The blood ran out of his body. He raised his eyes to me, his face twisted in horror, in disbelief. He tried to speak, but blood rolled over his tongue and bubbled over his lips.

He sank on his side to the grass, hugging himself. He bled out so quickly.

I stood there watching, fighting back my nausea, gritting my teeth. So quickly. It happened so quickly. Or was I standing outside time? Did it actually take him a long time to die?

I can't tell you, Diary. I stood and watched the spreading blood. Such a big puddle of his blood, with him curled on his side inside it.

I was still gasping for breath, fighting the deep shudders that paralyzed my body, when I knew he was dead.

And as soon as I knew, I started to move, to breathe again, to think more carefully and calmly.

I wiped the blood-soaked knife on the sleeve of his hoodie. Then I folded it up and tossed it into my bag. Gathered my belongings and stuffed everything back where it belonged.

Then I drove home, sobbing all the way. Sobbing at the top of my lungs, big tears rolling down my face, burning my cheeks.

My boyfriend, my only true love, was dead. I killed him. Stabbed him and watched him bleed to death. Killed him. I killed him.

So of course I cried. Cried and sobbed and moaned all the way home. I knew my life would never be the same.

PART
TWO

15.

Thankfully, Mom and Dad were asleep in their room. I couldn't have faced them. I would've collapsed in a heap and never moved again.

How could I explain to them what I did? I couldn't explain it to myself.

I stood in the dark kitchen without turning on a light. My bag suddenly felt as if it weighed a hundred pounds. I let it fall to the floor in front of the kitchen door.

The house was so still. The only sounds were my harsh breaths and the hum of the refrigerator. I took a few steps toward the kitchen counter. My sneakers squeaked on the tile floor. I pictured them covered in blood.

I pictured Blade swimming on his side in a lake of his own blood. I never knew that blood could smell so powerful. It smelled tangy and sour, very metallic.

I pictured Blade raising his head above the blood, gazing at me. Blood flowed down his face, thickly matted his hair. But he stared at me through the layer of blood, an accusing stare. He didn't need to speak. I could read the horror and the anger on his face.

I shook my head hard, erasing the terrifying picture from my mind. I shut my eyes tight and held them closed. Could I stay in this darkness and keep all these pictures from my brain?

No. For some reason, Deena Fear appeared before my eyes. Her black hair flew about her head as if being blown by a hurricane wind. Her lips were bright red, brighter than Blade's blood.

In my imagination, my feverish imagination, she raised a red hoodie in both hands and waved it at me.

Why is she doing that? Why is she even in my thoughts now?

The frightening stories of the Fear family contained many murders. According to legend, the Fears throughout their history knew how to murder people in the most hideous and painful ways.

But I'm a Donnelly. My grandparents came from County Wicklow in Ireland. We have never been murderers . . . till now.

I made my way through the dark house, then up the stairs to my room. I leaned on the banister and stepped as lightly as I could. I didn't want to make a sound.

I closed the bedroom door carefully behind me, crossed the room in the dark, and slumped onto the edge of my bed. The window was open. The curtains drifted in and out softly in a gentle breeze. Pale light from the street-light across the street washed over the carpet.

I sat hunched on the bed staring at the shadows of the shifting curtains. I don't know how much time passed. I didn't move. I barely breathed.

At some point, I scratched the fingernails of my left hand over the back of my right hand. Dug the nails into the skin. Just to feel something. Just to feel some pain. But I was numb. My hand was like a limp sponge. I didn't feel a thing.

I sat there staring at shadows, chilled in the breeze from the window. Images rolled through my mind. Red hoodies . . . rivers of blood . . . Blade's accusing eyes . . . I couldn't shut the pictures out.

"I have to confess," I said out loud, my voice hollow as it broke the deep silence. "I have to tell what I have done. I murdered Blade. I murdered him."

I collapsed into shoulder-heaving sobs. I lowered my head, covered my face with both hands, and cried. Cried till my face and hands were soaked from tears.

The flashing red-and-blue lights made me stop. I lowered my hands and stared at the glare of the lights outside the bedroom window.

I heard a car door slam. The sharp sound snapped me from my shock. I grabbed a wad of tissues and mopped my face. Then I stumbled to the window and gazed down at the street.

A Shadyside police patrol car had stopped at the bottom of my driveway. The flashing red-and-blue roof lights gave the front lawn an eerie, unreal carnival glow. I watched two dark-uniformed officers striding up the driveway.

My knees started to collapse. I gripped the windowsill to keep myself up. A wave of nausea made me swallow hard. Again. Again.

They were here. The police were already here. Here to arrest me for Blade's murder.

I lurched into the hall and flew down the dark stairs. So fast. The police were so fast. So quick to end my life.

16.

Gripping the banister tightly, I stopped at the foot of the stairs. The two cops stood side by side in the open front doorway. The pulsing red-and-blue lights behind them made them appear to flicker in and out of view.

They eyed me in silence as I stepped up to the doorway. They had their caps off. They both had short, black hair and dark eyes. They could have been twins, except that the one on the left was about a foot taller than his partner and had a thick black mustache.

The tall one had his right hand resting on the gun holster at his waist. They both stood erect, tense, as if expecting trouble.

I didn't plan to give them any trouble. I knew why they were there, and I knew I had no choice but to surrender to them.

I gazed from one to the other. Their faces revealed no emotion at all. I wondered if they could see how much I was trembling. "I-I . . . know why you're here," I stammered.

Their eyes grew wider as they studied me. "You do?" the shorter cop said.

His partner shifted his weight uncomfortably. "I'm Officer Rivera and he's Officer Miller. We were driving past and saw your front door open," he said. "We wanted to make sure no one had broken in."

My breath caught in my throat. I started to choke, but covered it up, made it sound like a cough.

I wanted to laugh. I wanted to do a crazy dance. I wanted to hug them both.

"Oh my God," I said, thinking fast. "My parents must have left it open. They . . . they were visiting friends. I think they just got home a little while ago."

The officers seemed as relieved as I did. Miller smiled and nodded. Rivera lifted his hand off his holster. He brushed back his short black hair.

"Or maybe it was the wind," I said, feeling braver. "I've been home all night. I didn't see the door was open."

"Check the latch," Miller said. "Make sure it works okay."

"Thanks for noticing," I said, my heart still racing. "I really appreciate it."

They started to turn away. But Rivera stopped and motioned to the sleeve of my shirt. I followed his gaze and saw the dark stain there.

My heart skipped a beat. I forced myself not to react at all.

"Is that blood?" he asked, studying it. "Did you cut yourself?"

I fingered the sleeve. Studied it, too. "It's an old stain," I said. "I don't think it's blood. I don't know what it is. It won't come out in the wash."

They both gave me two-fingered salutes, touching their foreheads. Then they turned and walked into the pulsing lights, down the front lawn to their car.

I closed the door carefully. I let out a long sigh of relief. My parents hadn't awakened. I leaned my back against the door, shut my eyes, and tried to force my heartbeats to slow.

They didn't come to arrest me for murder.

But they'd be back.

I opened my eyes and ran my fingers over the dark stain on my sleeve. Still damp.

"The knife!" Did I say those words out loud?

The bloodstain reminded me of the knife, and I realized I didn't remember what I had done with it.

The murder weapon.

In my horror, in my panic, in my insane moment of deadly rage—did I leave it beside Blade's body? Did I just toss it to the ground and run?

Or did I take it with me?

I suddenly pictured dropping it in my bag. My bag . . .

I'd left it by the kitchen door. Taking a deep breath, I pushed myself away from the front door and made my way to the kitchen. I grabbed the bag by the twin handles and carried it up to my room.

Holding the bag brought back all my panic, all the horror of that terrible scene beside Blade's house. The tug-of-war—Blade and I battling over this bag in my hands. . . . If only . . . If only I hadn't let go. If only Blade hadn't overturned the bag. . . .

The knife never would have fallen out. I never would have seen it or thought about it. . . . Or *used* it.

I heaved the bag onto my bed and bent to paw through it. Yes. There it was. It took only a few seconds to feel the knife at the bottom, to wrap my fingers around the handle, and lift it out. It trembled in my hand as if it were alive.

I held it in front of me and snapped it open. The silvery blade gleamed under the bedroom ceiling light, and tiny droplets of blood sparkled like jewels.

Blade's blood. I stared at the blade until I was nearly hypnotized by it. Stared at the glowing blood drops and the smear of blood near the handle. Stared until I wanted to scream. Until I wanted to explode.

Yes. I suddenly knew I would explode—just go to pieces in a furious burst of horrifying energy—if I didn't do something. If I didn't tell someone.

"I can't stand it." The words burst from my mouth. "I can't take it. I can't keep it all inside me."

I let the knife fall to the rug at my feet. But the sparkling blood droplets on the blade lingered in my eyes.

Before I exploded, I had to tell someone. I had to confess what I had done.

Julie. I thought immediately of my friend Julie. She was so practical, so sensible. She would listen to me. She wouldn't freak out.

I grabbed my phone in my trembling hand. The keypad came up. I stabbed at it, struggling to punch in Julie's number.

The phone rang twice before she answered.

"Julie? It's me!" I cried in a high, shrill voice. And the words just lurched from my mouth as if I were vomiting them into the phone. "I killed him! I did it. Oh, help me, Julie. Please help. I killed him. I just snapped. I lost it. I snapped. And I killed Blade!"

17.

I choked on the last words. My throat tightened and I couldn't speak. Panting, I pressed the phone to my ear.

"Who is this?" A hoarse voice on the other end, a woman's voice I didn't recognize. "Young lady, is this a prank call? If it is, it isn't funny."

Oh, wow. I glanced at my phone screen. Wrong number. I'd called a wrong number.

"S-sorry," I stammered. I clicked the call off before she could say anything else. I tossed the phone into my bag.

I dropped onto the bed and sat there hugging myself. I knew I wouldn't get to sleep that night. I wondered if I'd ever sleep again.

Blade's funeral was held in a small nondenominational chapel in North Hills. The chapel was long and narrow with dark wood-paneled walls and low wooden rafters overhead. Morning sunlight filtered in through narrow stained glass windows high on the walls.

Two huge vases of white lilies stood under spotlights in the front of a small altar. A podium stood between them. And beside the podium was Blade's coffin, made of shiny dark wood that glowed purple under the spotlights.

The coffin lid was up, and, from my seat near the back of the room, I could see that it was lined with a white satiny material. The idea that Blade was lying lifeless in that box didn't seem real to me.

Organ music played in the background. People drifted in silently. Not very many. Blade's family had moved to town so recently.

I sat between Julie and Miranda. Julie kept squeezing my hand and asking if I was okay. I nodded and wiped my tears with tissue after tissue.

I felt the whole thing was a dream. Staring at the tall flowers and the gleaming dark casket, the scene became a blur, and I knew I was about to wake up from this dream and go back to my real life. My real life with Blade.

But there were his parents in the front row, older-looking than I remembered. I'd only met them once. They huddled head to head, sobbing together, sobbing and shaking their heads as if they too didn't believe this could possibly be happening.

Miranda sneezed. The sound echoed off the low rafters. A few people turned around.

I gazed around and counted. Only nineteen or twenty people in the chapel. The pale, sad people dressed in dark colors squeezed together in the front two rows were relatives.

Julie, Miranda, and I were the only ones I recognized from our high school. I turned and let out a sharp breath as I saw Vanessa, the girl with white-blonde hair, the girl Blade took to the dance club. She came walking down the middle chapel aisle. She kept her eyes straight ahead on the coffin at the altar.

A few rows behind me, she turned. She saw me. She blinked. Stared for a moment, remembering. Then turned her gaze back to the front.

I felt my face start to burn as if on fire. *Did Vanessa know? She saw me go berserk at the club. Did she know?*

She walked right past my row and didn't glance my way again. She took a seat in the third row, behind the family, behind those who were sobbing and moaning and wiping their eyes.

I cried, too. The organ music rose, then fell. A young minister appeared, his head bowed solemnly. He had spikey dark hair and a black beard that he kept scratching as he gave his talk. He wore a brown sport jacket over dark slacks. His white shirt was open at the neck.

"Please sit down, everyone. We will begin. If you are new to this chapel, my name is Reverend Norman Preller." He had a soothing voice and spoke very softly into the podium microphone. The sound echoed off all the empty seats.

"I want to confess that I never had the pleasure of meeting Blade." Preller rubbed his beard. It made a scratchy sound in the loudspeakers. "But so many people have come to tell me what a fine young man he was, that I feel the pain of this tragedy almost as much as anyone who knew him."

Yes, it was a tragedy.

Julie handed me another tissue. I wadded up the old one and stuffed it into my lap. I stared at the open coffin, at the white satin lining of the lid, and my thoughts wandered. I couldn't listen to this soft-voiced minister who had never met the boy I loved.

I thought about the night Blade and I parked up at River Ridge, high over Shadyside. The river sparkled beneath us in the light of a full moon.

We got out of my car and spread a blanket on the grass. Then we lay there on our backs, holding each other and gazing up at the stars. It was such a clear, silver, magical night.

We held each other and kissed and talked and talked. We talked together so easily. It was as if we had been close for all our lives. Blade talked about how his dream was to be an archaeologist. He wanted to live out on the prairie and dig up dinosaur bones and discover things about the distant past that no one had ever known.

Funny. I said my life's ambition was to leave Shadyside. That was my only goal.

Blade teased me. He said my goal was too easy. He said we could leave Shadyside any time we wanted. "Let's take off together," he said, his lips brushing my cheek. "We could just leave a note for our parents and head west. How about Montana? We could go to Montana."

I laughed and poked him in the ribs. "Montana? Really? Why Montana?"

He raised a finger and poked me back. "Aren't you curious about Montana?"

"Uh . . . no," I said. "I've never thought about Montana."

"That's why we should go," he said. He pulled me close. "Or maybe we should just stay here forever."

That was an awesome night, a night I'll never forget. I knew Blade wasn't serious about taking off, but I didn't care. I thought maybe someday . . .

But now here I was in this dark, stuffy chapel. Instead of gazing at the stars, I was gazing at Blade's coffin. The sermon was over. Prayers were said. And now everyone was standing, and a line was forming to walk past the coffin to give a last goodbye.

Blade's parents stood against the wall. His mother had her face buried in a handkerchief. His father kept shifting his weight nervously, his face pale and grim. The relatives were the first to march past the coffin and offer their whispered condolences to the parents.

I held back. "I don't want to," I said.

Julie and Miranda took my arms. "You have to, Caitlyn," Miranda said. "You want to say goodbye, don't you?"

I had a sudden strong urge to confess. To tell them what I had done. I bit my tongue and forced the impulse down.

I joined the line to the coffin. Julie and Miranda stayed close behind me. At the front wall, Vanessa was shaking hands with Blade's parents, nodding her head solemnly. I couldn't hear what she was saying. She turned and started up the side aisle, heading to the chapel exit. She didn't look over at me.

It all seemed unreal again. I felt as if I was floating over everything, not on the floor, not in this chapel. I wanted to be a bird, my wings spread, flying high overhead, not tied to the earth, not part of this horrible scene.

Floating . . . floating . . . My heart pattering like a hummingbird heart.

And there I was, gazing into the satiny coffin, staring at Blade's lifeless face. It was Blade and it wasn't Blade. His face was smothered behind a layer of makeup. His cheeks a bright pink. His hair matted in a clump on his head.

And the eyes . . . the blank stare . . . the glassy eyes. Open. Why did they leave his eyes open?

I sucked in a breath and pulled back. I suddenly didn't want him to see me. I didn't want to see my face reflected in those fake glass eyes.

Someone moaned. I think it was Blade's mother. Someone behind me sobbed loudly.

Julie grabbed my arm. We started to move past the coffin. But I let out a startled cry—and stopped. I stopped and stared in horror as Blade blinked those glassy green eyes.

His head slid to the right, then the left. And then it began to raise itself off the white satin pillow.

I gasped and clapped my hands over my mouth. I grabbed onto Julie with both hands as my knees started to fold. I opened my mouth to scream but no sound came out.

Was I imagining it? Was it my guilt wishing him back to life?

No. The room rang with screams and shrieks of horror, choked gasps and moans of disbelief.

"*No . . . No . . . Noooo . . .*" Blade's parents howled and raised their hands high in front of them, as if shielding themselves from the horror. In the middle aisle, an older woman slumped in a dead faint to the floor. No one rushed to help her. All eyes were on the coffin.

All eyes were on the corpse, as slowly . . . as if in slow motion . . . slowly . . . Blade sat up.

18.

"He's moving! He's climbing out!"
"He's alive!"

"Blade—can you hear us? Blade?"

"Oh my God! This is impossible! This is crazy! Oh my God!"

Frightened voices rang out through the chapel. No one moved. Miranda and Julie had backed away from me. They huddled together at the side of the altar, their faces pale, eyes bulging.

I stood with my hands clamped to the sides of my face, frozen in front of the coffin, just a few feet from the moving corpse.

"A miracle! A miracle! My boy is alive!" his mother cried.

"A doctor. Is there a doctor here?" a woman shouted. "We need a doctor."

"He's alive! Get him out of there! He's not dead!"

Blade raised himself, his body stiff, his lips clamped tightly together, glassy eyes straight ahead. With his painted pink cheeks and lipsticked lips, he reminded me of a ventriloquist dummy. I suddenly felt like I was in one of those horror movies, the ventriloquist dummy coming to life, evil and menacing.

Of course, he was dead. I killed him. I watched him bleed out. I knew he was dead.

But here was Blade, my sweet dead Blade, sitting up in his pearly white coffin.

I watched his hand come up, so slowly, as if every inch was painful to him, as if every slight move was a challenge. Yes, Diary, his right hand slid up, and he turned his body. Twisted himself toward the horrified, paralyzed crowd of people who had come to mourn him.

The glassy eyes surveyed the crowd, moved from his parents to the middle-aged couple beside them to the older man leaning on a cane, all frozen in amazement, in disbelief.

He turned some more, a hard twist of his body. And now his eyes were on me. They had no pupils. They were solid green, the color of spring grass.

He trained his eyes on me and . . . and his lips trembled. His cheeks strained. He was trying to talk. Trying to open his mouth and talk. *But his lips were sewn together.*

He struggled and strained, mouth twisting into an ugly expression. Finally, he gave up. Eyes still on me, he raised his hand—and pointed. Pointed an accusing finger at me. The finger trembled in the air, then steadied itself, and he pointed me out to everyone.

I could almost hear his voice, almost hear him saying, "She killed me, everyone. She's the reason I'm a corpse."

"Ohhhhhhhh." A moan escaped my throat. I couldn't bear to face him. I knew I'd see those neon pink cheeks, those sewn-together red lips, the blank, blind eyes forever. Forever.

"Ohhh noooo." With another animal moan, I spun around to escape the horrifying sight. And saw a figure standing halfway up the aisle. A figure all in black.

Deena Fear.

Her straight black skirt came down nearly to the floor. She wore a black vest over a pleated, dark purple dress shirt. She stood in the aisle with her hands outstretched, curled into tight fists. And she was muttering, muttering something rapidly to herself.

Behind the owl-like glasses, her eyes were locked on the corpse.

She kept her fists tight and straight in front of her. In one fist, she carried some kind of silver ornament. An amulet, shaped like a bird with wings outstretched.

She held the amulet in front of her, tilted her head back, her lips moving rapidly. And I realized she was chanting, chanting words in a strange language, chanting under her breath, her face tight with concentration.

She raised the amulet above her head and the corpse moved. She swung her fists and the corpse swung its arm. She twisted the amulet up and down, and the corpse nodded its head.

It took me a long time to realize she was controlling him.

Chanting a little louder, she moved down the aisle toward us, her arms straight out, bird amulet gripped in front of her. She was breathing hard. Her eyes were tight slits. Her jaw was clenched in concentration.

Deena Fear brought Blade back to life.

"Deena!" I shouted her name. "Deena—what are you *doing?*"

She ignored my question and kept chanting, her lips moving rapidly, her eyes locked on the moving corpse. She took another step toward the coffin. She jerked her arms hard, and the corpse shuddered.

A hush fell over the chapel. Everyone watched Deena, watched the corpse, watched the horror show in amazed silence. The woman who had fainted was recovering in a pew at the side. Two little girls dressed in black hugged each other, crying loudly.

"Deena—" I called to her again.

"Come back, Blade," she murmured, stepping closer. "Come back now. Come back. Come back." Rivulets of sweat poured down her forehead and cheeks. The amulet trembled in her fist.

She raised her eyes to me. "Don't interrupt. This takes so much concentration . . . so much energy. I . . . I . . ."

I gasped as her eyes rolled up in her head. She uttered a short choking sound. Her knees collapsed. Her hands fell to her sides. And she collapsed onto the chapel floor.

Her head bounced hard against the wood. The amulet slid under a pew.

She didn't move.

Screams all around. I spun back to the coffin and didn't see Blade. I took a lurching step toward the alter, peered into the satiny casket lining, and saw him on his back. Eyes blankly staring up at the ceiling lights. Arms at his sides.

Dead again.

Not moving. Lifeless head sunk into the satin pillow. Not breathing. A corpse. A corpse. A corpse once again.

Blade's mother had collapsed to the floor, legs out-stretched, her back against the wall. Her husband was try-ing to get her to take a cup of water. But his hands were shaking so hard, he spilled it on her.

People were screaming. People were crying. Julie and Miranda hid themselves behind one of the tall lily vases. They were talking rapidly, both talking at once, both making wild gestures with their hands.

A doctor trotted to the altar. He gazed frantically around the chapel, unable to decide who to help first. People sat devastated in the pews. A man slumped at a side pew, holding his hand over his heart, groaning loudly.

The doctor dropped to his knees in the aisle and leaned over Deena Fear. He raised her wrist, feeling for a pulse.

I moved over to Julie and Miranda. The three of us did a group hug, holding onto each other as if trying to hold on to reality, the real world, the world we knew where corpses didn't sit up in their coffins. Julie wiped her eyes with a damp handkerchief. Her cheeks were red from tears.

I felt a lot of things all at once. Alert and tense. Waiting for the next impossible thing to happen. Numb. And mainly frightened.

The doctor rubbed Deena's limp hand between his hands. I heard Deena groan. He reached behind her back and guided her to a sitting position.

She blinked and shook her head. Her black hair had fallen over her face. She brushed it away with both hands. "So much energy . . ." she murmured.

The doctor said something to her, bringing his face down to her ear. I couldn't hear what he said. The chapel had been silent, but now everyone was talking at once.

The doctor stood up, brushed off the knees of his dark suit pants, and moved to the man in front who was still pressing a hand over his chest.

Blade's parents were clinging to the sides of the coffin now, staring down at their dead son. His mother whispered something to him. Was she hoping he would sit up again?

I shuddered. I watched Deena climb to her feet. She grabbed the back of a pew to steady herself. Her glasses were crooked. Her face was as white as paper, and her chin and lips were trembling.

She searched until she found the silver bird amulet. Then she carefully lifted it off the floor and tucked it into her pocket.

Reverend Preller suddenly reappeared. I hadn't seen

him since the funeral ceremony began. He kept blinking rapidly, and one cheek twitched. He adjusted the sleeves of his brown jacket and kept clearing his throat nervously as he stepped up to the podium.

"Ladies and gentlemen," he began. The roar of screams and cries drowned him out. He tapped the microphone a few times. "Ladies and gentlemen, please."

The room quieted. He cleared his throat again. Played nervously with the knot on his necktie. His cheek twitched some more. "We've had an unfortunate incident," he said.

Those words caused everyone to start talking again.

An unfortunate incident?

Preller's face reddened. He cleared his throat again. "I need to make this last announcement," he pleaded. "The . . . burial will be held as scheduled. All are invited to Shadyside Oaks Cemetery. The family has requested that I tell you there will be no reception afterward. They request that they be allowed to deal with this devastating loss in privacy."

"But he isn't *dead*!" someone shouted.

This caused another roar of voices. I realized I was pressing my hands over my ears. *I have to get out of here. I can't take anymore.*

Julie and Miranda were talking heatedly to Preller, both gesturing and motioning to the coffin. I decided I would talk to them later.

I started up the side aisle toward the back of the chapel. My chest felt heavy. It was hard to breathe. I needed fresh air. I needed to go somewhere and think. I needed to escape.

I was halfway up the aisle when I realized Deena Fear was watching me. I stopped and turned toward her. She mouthed some words I couldn't understand. She seemed to be pleading with me. Her expression was intense.

She cupped her hands around her mouth and shouted. But the voices ringing off the walls and low rafters were deafening. I couldn't hear her.

I gave her a quick wave. I didn't want to talk with her. I had to escape. I turned away and trotted up the rest of the aisle. I pushed open the doors with both hands and stepped into the sunlight.

The sudden brightness made me shield my eyes with one hand. I took a deep breath of the warm air. I saw a group of children laughing and chasing each other in a playground across the street.

A sob escaped my throat. I wanted to be there playing with them. I wanted to be a child again.

I took another breath and made my way down the concrete chapel steps. A young man in blue sweats and a red-and-blue Red Sox cap jogged past me, leading a small brown dog on a leash.

The sunlight felt warm on my face. I left my car at the curb and wandered around for a while. I was dazed, Diary. In shock. Everyone at the funeral must have felt as upset and off-balance and totally weirded out as I did.

After walking in circles around North Hills, I must

have gotten back in my car. I must have driven home. I don't remember the drive at all.

The next thing I knew I was in my driveway. And then walking into the kitchen through the back door. I grabbed onto the kitchen counter. I felt dizzy and nauseous.

"Mom? Dad?" I called out. But, of course, they were at work.

I suddenly realized I hadn't eaten all day. Maybe some food in my stomach would help calm me. I was on my way to the kitchen when my phone beeped.

I picked it up and gazed at the screen. A text message. I didn't recognize the phone number. I lowered my eyes to the message and read:

It's me. Deena. They didn't bury him. It's not too late.

19.

I stared into the glare of my phone screen. I read the message again. I knew what Deena meant. I didn't have to puzzle over it.

I pictured her standing so tensely in the chapel aisle, the bird amulet raised in front of her as she chanted, chanted, and concentrated. And made the corpse move. Made Blade sit up. Made him turn and point at me. Stare at me with those terrifying glass eyes.

And I knew what she wanted now. She wanted to finish bringing Blade back to life. She wanted to finish what she started in the chapel. But why? Why did she want to bring Blade back?

To find out who killed him? Did she believe if she brought him back, he would name his murderer? Namely *me*.

The thought made me shudder. The phone slipped from my hand and dropped onto the kitchen floor. And as I fumbled to pick it up, it beeped again.

And there was another text from Deena:

It's urgent. Come to my house NOW.

And then another text:

Don't think about it. U don't have a choice.

I set the phone down on the kitchen counter. I didn't want to hold it. I didn't want to read any more messages from Deena Fear.

"She's crazy," I murmured out loud. I opened the fridge, grabbed a bottle of orange juice, tilted it to my mouth, and gulped it down. When I finished, I was breathing hard, my chest heaving.

I loved Blade. At least, I thought I loved him. But I didn't want him back. I didn't want him alive again. Alive to tell everyone that I was a murderer, that I went into an insane rage and stabbed him, stabbed him, stabbed him.

I knew if Blade came back . . . If Deena really could bring him to life again . . . my life would be over.

How could I stop her from doing this? I didn't have a clue. I didn't know how to stop her. But I definitely didn't want to *help* her.

I grabbed a container of tuna salad from the fridge and began forking it into my mouth. I was starving. I felt as if I had a vast canyon inside me. It wasn't normal. I never get ravenous like this.

Nothing was normal now. Nothing.

People would be talking about the funeral forever. The corpse who sat up in his coffin. It would be on the news. It would be all over town . . . everywhere. A major news story—and a horrifying memory for everyone who was there.

I stared at Deena's text on my phone. I wanted to take the phone and heave it as far as I could out the back door. I wanted to be by myself. I didn't want anyone to reach me.

I jumped as the phone rang. Deena. She wasn't going to leave me alone. She wasn't going to give me a chance.

I let it ring for a long while till I couldn't stand it any longer. I swung it off the counter and pressed it to my ear. "Deena—leave me alone!" I cried.

Silence at the other end. Then: "Huh? Caitlyn? Is that you?"

"Julie?" I swallowed. "Oh, hi. I . . . thought it was a wrong number."

"Caitlyn, are you okay? You left the chapel without telling us. Miranda and I—"

"Sorry," I said. "I had to get out of there. It was all so weird and—"

"It was so freaky, Caitlyn," Julie said breathlessly. "When Blade's body started to move, I . . . I thought I was in a horror movie. I've never been so scared in my life."

"Me, too," I said.

"I couldn't even scream," Julie said. "I just held on to Miranda and watched. Everyone was screaming and fainting and crying and—"

"It was too horrible," I said. "Like a bad dream."

"No one could believe it," Julie said. "That minister . . . He was a total nerd, wasn't he? He tried to explain it. He said the floor was tilted and the coffin moved—not the body. He was trying to reassure everyone, I guess."

"That's stupid," I said. My stomach growled. I opened the fridge and looked for something else to eat.

"We're not stupid. We saw what happened, Caitlyn. Right? It wasn't the coffin tilting. Blade sat up. He was dead but he sat up and he tried to talk." Her voice cracked. I heard her coughing.

He tried to talk and tell everyone that I killed him.

"Julie? Are you okay?" I asked.

"No, I'm not okay. I'll never be able to get it out of my mind. I'll always see him sitting up in the coffin, straining and struggling. I'll always see those weird green eyes. His hand slowly raising. I'll never be able to forget it. I . . . I think I'm going crazy, Caitlyn. Do you really think Deena Fear made him sit up?"

"I don't know," I said. "Maybe. She's a Fear, right? That family is supposed to know about all kinds of magic. Dark, frightening magic. You've heard the stories, too. We all have. How some of them had strange powers. I mean . . . that amulet she held . . ."

"And she was chanting something. Oh my God, Caitlyn. Do you really think she made him sit up?"

"I don't know. Maybe. Maybe she did. It's too frightening to talk about, Julie. We have to try to get past it somehow." Those words sounded phony, even as I said them.

Why didn't I tell Julie about the urgent texts from Deena, how Deena said it wasn't too late? I don't know.

Maybe I thought if I didn't tell anyone about Deena, she would go away. The whole thing would go away.

"They didn't bury him, Caitlyn," Julie said. "The body is still in the chapel. Blade's parents wouldn't let them bury him. They were totally messed up. They were screaming and crying. It was horrible."

"What do you mean? What happened?"

"They wouldn't leave the coffin. They grabbed Blade's body and began to shake it. They said it might come alive again. They said he wasn't really dead. They saw him sit up. Everyone saw him. And they wouldn't let him be buried in case he moved again."

"Oh, wow. Oh, wow."

"There was a doctor there, remember? You saw him. He revived Deena Fear when she fainted? Well . . . he managed to get Blade's parents to step aside. It wasn't easy. Finally, he examined the body.

"And what did the doctor say?" I asked.

"He said Blade was dead. Not breathing. The parents both started screaming for him to go away. And then that minister Preller started shouting for everyone to leave. He threatened to call the police if everyone didn't leave the chapel right away."

"Oh, wow. Then what happened?"

"It got way ugly. Blade's parents grabbed the sides of the coffin and said they would never leave. Preller tried to pull them away. It started to be a real fight. Miranda and I . , . we hurried out of there. I couldn't stand it anymore, and I didn't want to be there when the police arrived. It was so *horrible*, Caitlyn."

"Oh, wow." I didn't know what to say. It was so hard to imagine . . .

"Poor Miranda," Julie continued. "She threw up on the sidewalk as soon as we got outside. She just heaved up her guts. She felt totally sick. She went straight home, and I . . . well . . . I wandered around for a while. In a total daze. I mean, I still feel sick and weird, and I can't stop the shakes. I mean, it's like it all followed me home."

"Julie, I feel the same way," I said.

"Do you want to come over?"

I thought about it. "No. Sorry. I think I'm going to try to take a nap. Maybe if I sleep for a while, I can calm myself down a little."

"Oh. Okay. Call me later. When you wake up. Okay?"

"Okay," I said. I clicked off.

I knew I was lying. I knew I wasn't taking a nap. I was driving to Deena Fear's house.

Why?

That I couldn't tell you.

20.

Shadows swallowed my car as I turned off Old Mill Road onto Fear Street. Tall, ancient trees on both sides had formed an archway over the street. Sunlight struggled to get through the tangled branches.

Fear Street winds along the east side of Shadyside. Large, old houses, mostly stone and brick, line one side of the street. Most of them are far back from the street, sitting on wide front yards, hidden by tall, well-trimmed hedges.

These are the oldest houses in town. They were built by rich settlers in the late nineteenth and early twentieth century, including the notorious Fear family (who were thought to practice strange dark magic.)

The houses all face the Fear Street Woods, a thick tangle of tall, old maple, sycamore, and oak trees, deep silent woods that stretch for miles, and, some say, are always in shadow. That's one of the many legends about the street. That the sun refuses to shine on the Fear Street Woods.

So many dark stories.

Everyone in town knows about the frightening animal howls in the woods late at night. The strange, darting creatures spotted by hunters, creatures running on two legs that no one could identify. And the two Fear sisters who, many years ago, were found dead in the woods with their bones all missing. Just their skin and organs resting under a tree. No bones.

Yuck. This is what I thought about, Diary, as I drove under the tall, arching limbs over Fear Street, looking for Deena Fear's house. Fear Street looks so normal and peaceful—even pretty—as you follow its curves. But most people in town, even those who are not superstitious, avoid it if they can.

I slowed the car near the end of the street as the ruins of the Fear mansion came into view. Over a hundred years ago, the magnificent old house burned to the ground in a tragic blaze, a fire that consumed the whole house and everyone in it.

Many said it was the evil in the house that caused the fire. It was reported that the screams inside the burning house lasted for hours—and continued long after the fire had been quenched.

That was over a hundred years ago. To this day, no one has cleared away the charred wreckage of the house. There has been no one willing to clear it or to build a new house on the evil site. The black-and-burned mansion hunches on its sloping lawn like some kind of giant broken insect.

A large stone guesthouse behind the mansion, nearly hidden at the edge of the woods, is where Deena Fear lives. I parked my car on the street. The driveway curving up to the mansion was overrun by tall weeds and burned pieces of lumber.

As I made my way up the lawn past the wreckage of the mansion, a blast of wind from the woods nearly blew me over. I toppled backward, trying to keep my balance. It was almost as if I was being warned to stay back, to not come any closer.

Why *was* I there? Why had I obeyed Deena's summons and hurried here when everything told me to avoid her, to stay away. Every sign screamed *danger*. So why did I hurry to this forbidden spot to see this strange girl who wasn't even a friend? Far from a friend.

I couldn't tell you. I couldn't explain it.

I ducked my head, holding my hair down with both hands as another strong gust howled past me. I stepped around a deep pile of ashes and had to jump over a tall clump of weeds.

The house was two stories high, very long, bigger than it appeared from the street. Several windows were shuttered. The others were all dark. The walls were a gray stone. The slanting shingled roof was painted red. The door at the side of the house appeared to be the only door.

I raised my hand to knock—and the door swung open.

Deena stood in the doorway. I heard classical piano

music from the room behind her. "Come in." She stepped aside. She didn't seem at all surprised to see me.

She hadn't changed from the funeral. Same pleated purple shirt, black vest, long black skirt almost to the floor. She had tied her long hair back with a black velvet ribbon. She had a tiny silver spider in one pierced nostril.

I followed her from the narrow front hall to a large living room. The rooms were all dark. One table lamp sent a dim gray light over the leather couch. The piano music grew louder. Two large painted portraits, an old-fashioned-looking man and woman, attractive but stern, cold-faced, unsmiling, faced the fireplace.

"My famous ancestors," Deena murmured. She motioned for me to keep walking.

The hall led past a library. Sunlight filtered in through a high, narrow window. I saw floor-to-ceiling bookshelves filled with old books, a desk piled high with books, a stack of books on the floor.

I couldn't resist. "Do you like to read?" I asked.

"Yes. But those books aren't for everyone," she answered. "You have to be interested in special things to want to read those books."

"Like what?"

She didn't answer. We turned a corner. I gazed down the long hall. "Are we all alone here?"

"No. My parents are here, too."

The hallway led to a large room at the back of the

house. I blinked in the sudden light. The back wall was glass, looking out into the woods.

Outside the window, tall weeds bent from side to side close to the house. A patch of spring wildflowers caught my eye. Beyond them, I saw a thick clump of evergreen shrubs.

I heard a *squawk*.

I blinked when I saw a parrot on a perch near the center of the room. "That's Tweety," Deena said. "He's my favorite. Isn't he a pretty boy?"

The bird was beautifully plumed with red, blue, and green feathers. It hopped on the perch, as if it was excited to see us. It squawked again, making sure we were paying attention.

My eyes caught a large aquarium on a table near the parrot perch. A single bed stood against the far wall. A desk with a laptop computer. A long, cluttered worktable, test tubes, glass pipes, like a chemist's table, scattered papers, electronic equipment I didn't recognize.

"This is my room," Deena said. "We can start here."

"Start what?" I asked.

Again, she didn't answer. She strode to the worktable and picked something up. When she turned, I saw that it was the silver bird amulet she had held at the chapel.

She raised it so I could see it clearly. Then she stepped back into the circle painted on her floor. "We don't have much time, Caitlyn." Behind the owlish glasses, her dark eyes stopped on me. "If we want to do this . . ."

"Deena—I don't understand," I said. "You have to tell me what you want to do."

She rolled her eyes. "Bring Blade back, of course."

My mouth dropped open. I started to protest, but no sound came out.

Deena spun the amulet in her hand. "I came close in the chapel," she said. "You saw. You saw how close I came. But it takes so much concentration. It takes so much out of me."

I couldn't hold back. "Are you for real?" I cried. "You made the corpse sit up. But you don't really think you can bring Blade totally back to life—do you?"

"Caitlyn, you saw the books in the library. The books told me how to do it. My family—we know things. We can do things."

"This is crazy," I said. "I'm sorry. I have to go. I don't know why I came."

"I do," she said, moving to block the doorway. "You came because you want to help me."

"N-no," I stammered. "That's not true. I don't want to help you. Because it's crazy, Deena. If you're serious, you need help. If you seriously think you can bring Blade back to life . . ." My voice faded. I was trembling.

She took a few steps toward me, lowering the amulet to her side. "If I prove it to you?"

"Huh? Prove it?" My head was swimming now.

"If I prove I can do it, will you help me? I don't have

the strength to do it alone. Will you help me if I prove I can do it?"

"No. You can't prove it," I said. "I'm sorry, Deena. This is too disturbing. You have to find someone to talk to. You're not making sense. I can't help you. I'm really sorry."

I started to the door. Deena grabbed my elbow and spun me around. "Watch. I can do it. I'm not crazy, Caitlyn. I'm a Fear. I can do terrible things. I can do frightening things. You have to believe me. Watch."

"Deena, wait—"

She grabbed the parrot around its middle. The bird squawked in surprise. She squeezed her fingers around it and swung it off its perch.

"Deena—stop!" I cried. "What are you going to do?"

The parrot squawked and twisted its head, struggling to escape. Deena carried it to the aquarium—and plunged the bird down into the water. Pushed it to the bottom and held it underwater.

"Deena—no! What are you doing?"

I rushed at her. I grabbed her arm. I tried to pull the bird up from the aquarium. But Deena pushed down with all her strength, and I couldn't move it.

"What are you *doing*?" I cried. "What are you doing?"

"Drowning the parrot," she said.

21.

The bird struggled, kicking its claws, twisting its head. Deena pressed it to the aquarium bottom.

I leaped back in horror. The water tossed and splashed. A few seconds later, it was still.

The parrot slumped in Deena's hand. She pulled it up. Water dripped off the beautiful feathers. It didn't lift its head. It didn't move.

"The parrot is dead," Deena said without any emotion at all. She squeezed the bird like a sponge, and water ran off it into the aquarium.

At that moment, at that horrifying, sickening moment, I realized how dangerous Deena was. And at the same time, I realized that I could be in danger, too.

She wasn't just crazy. She could take a beautiful bird—her pet, her favorite—and drown it in her hand and *not feel anything.*

I gripped my throat. I felt sick.

"Now watch," Deena snapped angrily. "Are you

watching, Caitlyn? What's wrong with you? I'm show-ing you something."

"Sorry," I said. My eyes were on the door. I didn't want to look at the dead bird. I pictured it in her hand, at the bottom of the aquarium. Struggling. Twisting and strug-gling. Little eyes bulging. Filling its lungs with water. Taking its last breath.

Deena set the parrot down on the worktable. Water rolled off its body, forming a puddle around it. She raised the silver amulet in front of her. She pressed it against the belly of the bird.

I took a deep breath and forced myself to breathe nor-mally.

Deena was chanting now, repeating and repeating words in a language I'd never heard before. She shut her eyes and held the amulet over the parrot. And chanted, her lips moving rapidly, the words repeating so softly I couldn't hear them.

Sweat formed on Deena's forehead. Her eyeglasses ac-tually steamed up. The amulet quivered in her hands as she continued to chant. A ray of sunlight through the window made the silver bird ornament glow.

I gasped when the parrot uttered a weak cry. The bird opened its eyes. It raised its head.

Deena continued to chant. Sweat ran down the sides of her face. Her voice became brittle, raspy.

The parrot uttered another squeak. It shook its head

hard, tossing off water. It tested its wings, then climbed unsteadily to its feet.

Deena stopped chanting and opened her eyes. She mopped her perspiring face with the sleeve of her shirt. Gently, she lifted the parrot off the table and returned it to its perch.

She brushed its wing feathers tenderly with one finger. The parrot tilted its head and nibbled at her finger.

Then Deena raised her face to me with a strange, pleased smile on her face. "Back to life," she said in a whisper.

I couldn't hide my shock. My mouth hung open as I stared at the parrot, preening its still-wet feathers. I struggled to think of what to say.

"I . . . I still want to go home," I said finally. "You are scaring me, Deena. I don't need this."

Her strange, tight-lipped smile returned. "Yes, I'm scary. That's why you're going to help me, Caitlyn."

"I-I don't understand," I stammered.

"You don't have to," she snapped. "Don't try to understand. Just come with me. We don't have much time."

"To bring Blade back to life?" My voice came out tiny. Fear tightened my throat.

She nodded. "They didn't bury him. He's still in the chapel. We have to go there now." She stepped away from the parrot perch. "You saw what I can do. We have to do it before it's too late."

"But . . . why?" I said. "Why bring him back, Deena?"

The parrot suddenly spoke up: "*Why? Why? Why?*"

Deena's eyes widened behind her large, round glasses. Circles of pink appeared on her pale cheeks. "Because I saw him first."

I gasped. "Huh? What does that mean? That doesn't make any sense."

"I saw him first, Caitlyn, and now it's my turn." She started to the door. "This time he'll be mine."

"Deena, wait," I said, hurrying after her. "Wait. I'm not doing this. I can't. I don't want to bring Blade back."

She wheeled around, and her eyes bulged with anger. "Why not? I thought you loved him. I thought you were crazy about him."

"I . . . I thought so, too," I said, my voice cracking. "But no. I can't do it. I don't want him back. It can't happen because—"

I stopped. I was about to confess why I didn't want to see Blade back. I was about to tell her that I was the one who killed Blade. And if he comes back . . . if he comes back . . .

I don't know what Blade will do to me, and I'm too terrified to find out.

I was about to confess. I was about to explain. I hesitated. I stood there debating, thinking hard. I didn't want to confide in this strange, frightening girl. What would she do if she learned the truth about me, the truth about Blade's murder?

I knew I couldn't tell Deena the truth. I knew I had to get away from her.

I took a deep breath, spun to the door, and took off. I raised both hands and shoved her out of my way.

Startled, Deena uttered a cry and staggered back a few steps, off-balance just long enough for me to escape. My shoes pounded the hard floor as I burst into the hallway, glanced right, then left.

Which way? Which way had we come in?

Shouting my name, Deena came running into the hall. I spun around and bolted to the right. The dimly lit hall gave me no clue as to the right direction to run.

I passed rooms on both sides, their doors shut tight. A high window at the end of the hall let in a wash of gray evening light. It made me feel as if I was running in a fog.

A mirror to my right gave me a glimpse of myself as I ran past, disheveled and frightened. At the end of the hall, another long corridor led in both directions.

I took the right again. I remembered there was only one door to this strange, old guest house. Was I running to it—or away from it?

Deena's shouts followed me, ringing off the walls, repeating my name again and again.

A sharp pain stabbed my side. I pressed my hand against it and kept running. The hall ended in black double doors. Not the entrance. I must have run the wrong way. And now I was trapped back here. Unless . . .

I grabbed both door knobs and swung the doors open. I could see a large dark room, the darkness cut by two slender beams of light from the high ceiling.

Deena's cries in my ears, I slammed the doors behind me. I fumbled for a lock on them. But no. I couldn't find any.

Gasping for breath, I staggered into the inky shadow of the room. I gazed up at the twin beams of light. So mysterious. And then I followed the light down . . . down . . . straight down to the floor.

I opened my mouth in a choked cry.

And gaped at the twin glass display cases. Tall glass cases rising up from the floor, glowing under the lights. And inside the cases . . .

Oh my God.

Two people. A man and a woman. Dressed in black outfits, as if for a funeral. Standing very still. Eyes wide. Each one staring out of a display case, staring straight ahead, not at each other.

The man had short, black hair and dark eyes. The woman had shoulder-length brown hair and bright blue eyes. Their faces were a strange orange.

Store mannequins, I thought. *Clothing store mannequins.*

But why were they here? Why hidden in a back room? Mannequins in glass cases with spotlights on them as if they were on display?

Still struggling to catch my breath, I took a few steps closer. The man's hands were at his sides. The backs of his hands were wrinkled, like real human hands. The woman had a diamond wedding ring on her left hand.

Behind me, the doors swung open with a crash. I gasped and spun around.

Deena stood in the doorway, holding onto the sides of the doors. Her gaze went from me to the twin cases. Then she locked her eyes on me.

"I see you've met my parents," she said.

22.

I opened my mouth to speak, but no sound came out. I stared at her open-mouthed, my legs trembling so hard I started to fall.

Finally, I found my voice. "That's a joke, right? You're joking?"

She shook her head. "Not a joke. That's Mom and Dad. In the flesh."

"But how?" I uttered. "I mean, why? I mean—"

"They never should have let me take that taxidermy class," she said.

I'm in a nightmare.

That's what I thought, Diary.

I turned my back on the display cases. I couldn't bear to look at them now. I pressed a hand to my throat, struggling to keep my lunch down.

"They are mannequins, right?" I said. "I know the stories about your family, Deena. But no way. *No way* I'll believe that you stuffed your own parents."

"I don't have time to explain," she said. "They were very annoying people. I didn't really have a choice."

She grabbed my hand and pulled me back into the hall. I must have been dazed or in shock or something. I let her pull me back to her room without a fight.

The parrot bobbed up and down on his perch, excited to see us again. The tall weeds outside the wide window swayed in a shifting breeze.

"You're going to help me, Caitlyn," Deena said softly. She removed her glasses and rubbed her eyelids. Her eyes looked so much smaller without her glasses. "You don't have a choice."

I didn't reply, just glared at her. The faces of the couple in the glass cases lingered in my mind. The woman *did* look a lot like Deena.

"You're coming to the chapel with me now," Deena said, her voice low and steady. "We're going to bring Blade back."

"No. I can't," I finally found my voice. "I can't bring him back. I don't *want* to bring him back."

And then, suddenly, I told her. It just came out of me.

"Deena, I don't want to see Blade again," I said. "I *can't* see Blade again. Because . . . because I'm the one who killed him."

Deena dove forward and grabbed me by the shoulders.

She gave me a hard shake. A disgusted sneer spread over her face.

"You idiot!" she cried. "*You're* not the one who killed him. *I* did!"

23.

Ashuddering cry escaped my lips. She gave me a shove, and I stumbled back a few steps. I caught my balance, but my head was spinning.

I stared at her, sucking in breath after breath.

Deena's hair was wild about her head now, as if it had come alive. Her normally pale face was red, her mouth in a tight scowl.

Was she lying? She had to be.

"You—you were there?" I choked out. "In Blade's backyard? When . . . when I stabbed him?"

"I stabbed him," she insisted. She crossed her arms in front of her black vest. "I mean, I *made* you stab him. You didn't act on your own, Caitlyn. You . . . you were too much in love with him to kill him."

She couldn't control her jealousy. She spat those last words, her face tight with fury.

"But—why?" I demanded. "Why kill him? Why did he have to be killed?"

"Because he betrayed us," Deena replied, arms still tightly crossed in front of her.

Us.

"I followed you to Blade's house that night," Deena said. She swept back her hair with both hands. "I couldn't let him get away with it. I didn't know . . . I didn't know he had a girlfriend. That girl Vanessa with the sweet smile and the mousy-soft voice. I wanted to puke, Caitlyn. Seriously. I just wanted to puke."

Behind me, Tweety the parrot chimed in again: "*Why? Why? Why?*"

"So . . . you followed me?" I said.

Deena nodded. "I waited and watched. I saw how angry you were at him. Angry and hurt. And you had every right to be, Caitlyn. I saw him first. I saw Blade first. But you had every right to be out-of-your-mind angry. And when I saw that knife fall out of your bag . . ."

Her voice trailed off. I could see Deena was picturing the whole thing in her mind as she described it to me.

"I saw my opportunity, and I took it," she said, eyes flashing behind the big eyeglasses.

"You're crazy," I blurted out. "Earth calling Deena. How about a little reality check? You didn't do anything. I picked up the knife. I held the knife. I stabbed him. I stabbed him and I killed him, Deena. Not you."

She crossed her arms again and smirked at me.

"I stabbed him! I stabbed him!" I shouted. The words came out in sobs. My whole body shuddered. I was finally confessing. Finally letting my horrible secret out. "I stabbed him and stabbed him!"

She shook her head. "Why are you such a pain? Didn't I tell you we have to hurry to bring Blade back?"

I wiped tears off my cheeks. I clenched my jaw, trying to stop the shudders that shook my body.

"Here's a quick demonstration," Deena said. "Here is how I made you stab Blade, okay? I was in charge. You weren't. I'll show you, Caitlyn."

I narrowed my eyes at her. "Another demonstration?" I shuddered and pictured her drowning the parrot again.

She pointed to the glass wall at the back of the room. Outside, I could see the late afternoon sun lowering behind the trees. Tiny white butterflies fluttered over the wildflowers at the back of the house.

Deena snapped her fingers, then worked them in some kind of code, almost like sign language. Then she pointed to the window again. "Go over there and do a cartwheel," she said.

"Okay," I said.

The parrot slid from side to side on his perch. I strode to the wall, stepped into a square of red sunlight on the floor, raised my arms above my head, and did a fairly graceful cartwheel.

I landed unsteadily and nearly stumbled into the glass. But I caught my balance and turned to Deena.

"Do another one," she said, motioning again with her fingers.

"No problem," I said. I concentrated this time and did a much more athletic cartwheel. This time I landed perfectly. "Ta-da."

"Are you catching on?" Deena said. "Are you starting to see how I can make you do whatever I want? Do you see how I used you to stab Blade?"

I felt confused. "Well . . ."

"I'll give you one more demonstration," she said. "If that's what it takes to convince you I'm telling the truth." She did that thing with her fingers again. "Caitlyn, go over there, take the parrot, and drown him again."

"Okay," I said.

24.

The parrot flapped his wings rapidly, ducked, and twisted his head. He seemed to sense what was coming. I wrapped my hand around his middle and lifted him off the perch. He squawked frantically and snapped his beak, trying to bite my hand as I carried him over to the aquarium.

I curled my hand tightly so he couldn't escape. I glimpsed six or seven goldfish in the tank, swimming slowly in a cluster. I lowered the parrot toward the water.

The bird began to squawk like crazy, squirming and twisting frantically in my hand.

"Okay, stop," Deena called. "Put Tweety back on his perch."

I turned away from the aquarium and quickly obeyed. I set the parrot down carefully on the perch. He squawked and nodded his head several times, as if telling me off.

"Tweety has had a tough day already," Deena said. "Let's give the dude a break."

I blinked. The room darkened as the sun dropped behind the trees. Somewhere far in the distance, I heard a howl. A hunting dog maybe.

Deena stood in the doorway. I could see the impatience on her face. She was waiting for me to say something.

"I understand," I said. "I get it, Deena." I let out a long sigh. "I see what you did. Mind control, right? You used me."

"It was for your own good," she replied.

My mouth dropped open. "Huh? My own good? Are you *kidding* me? You . . . you turned me into a *murderer*."

"He betrayed us," she said. "He had it coming." She turned and headed into the hall.

"But what about my life?" I cried, hurrying after her. "My life might be over. I'm a murderer. If the police figure it out . . . If they arrest me . . ."

"It will be different this time," she said, picking up her pace, jogging to the door, her hair flying behind her.

"Slow down, Deena. You're not listening to me at all." We passed the library with all the old, dust-covered volumes from floor to ceiling, books of evil magic, I decided, witchcraft, voodoo, supernatural spells. . . . I'm sure Deena was familiar with it all.

"It will be different," she said, grabbing car keys from a basket on a table in the front entryway. "This time he'll be mine. This time he will treat me right. It's going to be awesome. Awesome, Caitlyn. You'll see."

She's totally insane, I thought. *She's in her own world.*

And here I was, going with her. Climbing into the little Honda Civic beside her. Fastening my seat belt. Preparing . . . for *what?*

"Deena, are you controlling me right now?" I demanded.

She started the car. Adjusted the mirror outside her window, shifted into reverse, and started to back down the weed-choked obstacle course of a driveway.

"Are you?" I asked. "Are you controlling me?"

"Going to be awesome," she repeated. The car bumped over something hard in the driveway. "You'll see. So different this time."

"But what are we *doing?*" I screamed. "Tell me. What are we doing right now? Where are we going?"

She backed off the driveway onto Fear Street. Across the street, the trees shivered in the woods. Long evening shadows fell over our car as she shifted into drive and sped off.

"We're going to the chapel, like I told you," she answered finally. "Blade is waiting for me. Waiting for me to bring him home."

I watched the smile spread across her face. "You're going to take him from his coffin and—"

"Bring him home and bring him back, back to life. Just like Tweety, my sweet parrot. I've already done the prep work, Caitlyn. I spent the whole night preparing. I've done everything the book said. I know I can do it. I have no doubt at all."

The houses rushed past us as she sped along Division Street. The evening rush hour traffic was mostly going the other way. I wanted to roll down the window and shout to the other cars: "Help me! Help me out of here!"

But instead, I tilted my head back against the seat and shut my eyes. I couldn't control my leaping thoughts. And I told myself I had only me to blame for this.

Why did I obey her text message and come running to her house? I could have avoided all the horrifying insanity—the drowned parrot, the dead parents under their spotlights. . . .

Perhaps she used her mind control powers to bring me to Fear Street and her house.

Perhaps I was never in control today.

From all the insanity, there was only one good thing I learned. I am not a murderer. Deena was the murderer. I wasn't in control.

Of course, the police would never buy that story. No one would. Knowing I wasn't responsible should have made me feel better. But here I was, a prisoner of this crazy girl, one more victim of the Fear family's evil, about to break into a chapel and steal a corpse from its coffin.

How could I possibly feel anything but fear and regret?

Deena pulled to the curb and parked the car near the corner. The little chapel stood in deep shadow now, the sun having completely gone down. Through the passenger window, I could see a pale sliver of moon hanging low over the trees.

A wide concrete path cut through the closely trimmed lawn. Deena made me lead the way. I guess, to make sure I didn't try to escape again.

We were halfway up the path when the front chapel door swung open.

"Quick!" Deena grabbed me and pulled me behind a wide evergreen shrub. We both ducked low and watched as Reverend Preller, still in that brown sport jacket, stepped out of the chapel. He turned and locked the door carefully. Then he raised his face to the sky. I think he was just taking a breath of the cool night air.

Deena pulled me down lower. The evergreen branches prickled my face. I couldn't see the minister now, but I heard his footsteps on the path. Growing louder. Coming closer.

My heart started to pound. If he turned in our direction, he would see us crouching there. We would be caught. And how would we explain what we were doing there?

He walked right past us. His eyes were on the sky. He walked quickly, whistling to himself, swinging his arms in a steady rhythm.

I turned and watched him reach the curb. He crossed the street and stepped up to a dark green car parked there.

Deena and I waited till he drove away. Then we straightened up and walked to the chapel entrance. "It's locked," I said. "We watched him lock it."

"Not a problem," she said softly. She motioned to the side of the building. "There's a back entrance behind the minister's office. I made sure it was unlocked before I left the funeral."

I followed her around the side. An orange light flickered dimly through the row of stained glass windows, a dim light inside. The back door was nearly hidden by tall shrubs.

Deena grabbed the door handle and tugged. The door slid open easily. We slipped inside. The air was hot in here and smelled stale.

We were in a back hallway. The door to Preller's small office was open. In the dim light, I could see a narrow desk piled high with papers, a laptop, and a stack of books.

And what were those things on top of the bookshelf? I squinted hard. *Star Wars* figures. The minister had a collection of *Star Wars* figures.

The floor creaked beneath our shoes. The sound brought me back from my wandering thoughts. I grabbed Deena's shoulder. "Do you think anyone's watching the chapel?" I whispered. "A night guard or something?"

She shrugged. "I don't know. Stay alert."

Alert? I'd never been more alert in my life. That's what fright can do to you. Every creak of the floor made me jump. Every flicker of the light made my heart skip a beat.

"It's about time for a cat to jump out at us and scare us

to death," I whispered. "Isn't that what always happens in these scary situations?"

Deena turned and glared at me. "Why are you making jokes? This isn't funny."

"I-I," I stammered. "My brain is trying to keep it light, I guess. That's one way of dealing with fear."

"Just shut up," she snapped. "Follow me."

A narrow doorway led us into the chapel. We were standing a few feet behind the altar. I let my eyes wander to the back of the long room. Electric candles along the walls sent a warm yellow glow over the empty pews, and up to the low wood-beam rafters.

The huge vases of lilies hadn't been moved. But the coffin was no longer resting between them. The sick-sweet smell of the lilies overwhelmed everything.

"There's no one here," Deena whispered. She pointed to a narrow side room in the corner. I followed her gaze and saw the dark wood coffin. Blade's coffin. The lid was down. The coffin was bathed in a deep blackness.

"They just moved it aside," Deena whispered. "Follow me. And do exactly as I say. We have to lift him out of the coffin carefully. Once he's out, we'll wrap our arms around his waist and walk him out between us."

I shivered. I'd never touched a dead person before. Blade was only the second dead person I'd ever seen. My grandmother was the first, and she was over eighty when she died.

Deena stepped up to the side of the coffin. I hung back. A wave of terror washed over me. What would the corpse feel like? Would it be all squishy and soft? Or had it hardened stiff as a board? Would it smell? Didn't all dead things smell horrible?

"What are you waiting for?" Deena motioned impatiently for me to join her.

I took a deep breath and stepped up beside her. The coffin rested on a low table. The lid was at my shoulders. I held my breath. I didn't want to smell it.

"It's . . . too dark," I whispered. "How can we see anything?"

Deena pulled out her phone. She clicked on the flashlight icon. The phone sent a bright narrow beam of white light over the coffin.

"Okay," she whispered. "Let's lift the lid together. It's probably not that heavy."

I moved my two hands to the edge of the lid. Deena held the phone light in her teeth and wrapped her hands on the lid.

"Okay. Now," she whispered.

I was shaking so hard, I didn't know if I could get my arms to move. But somehow I found the strength. We both pushed up. The lid lifted easier than I imagined.

We raised the lid high, and it clicked into place in an upright position. Then we lowered our arms, took a step back, both breathing noisily. Deena aimed the light into the coffin. It made the white satin lining glow.

We stared into the light—and both uttered sharp cries that echoed off the rafters.

The coffin was empty.

Blade was gone.

25.

"Caitlyn, can we talk to you?"

I stared at the two cops who stepped up to my car. I recognized them immediately. Rivera and Miller. They had come to my front door a short while after I had stabbed Blade.

Now here they were at the mall, studying me as I climbed out of my car. I had hoped to go to my job. My nice normal boring job behind the popcorn counter.

But . . . no way.

They motioned to their patrol car. My whole body shuddered with dread as I lowered myself into the back-seat.

At the Shadyside precinct house, Rivera and Miller led me into a small square interview room. I gazed around the room, my hands clasped in front of me, my jaw clenched tightly. I was determined not to show how terrified I was.

What do they know?

In the patrol car on the way here, they told me they just had a few questions for me. They read my rights to me. Just like on *Law & Order.* They said I had the right to have my parents and a lawyer present.

That was the *last* thing I wanted.

"Are you arresting me?" I asked, my voice tiny and choked.

Rivera shook his head. "Just a few questions, that's all. A few things to clear up."

I'm guilty, I thought. *How much do you know? Do you know I'm the one who stabbed him?*

"Want us to call your parents?" Miller asked.

"No," I repeated. "It isn't necessary. I mean . . . if it's just a few questions."

The walls of the interview room were a sick pea soup green, and the paint was peeling near the ceiling. Two lights inside gray cones hung down over a long table. The tabletop was covered in names and initials carved into the wood. The windowless room was hot and smelled of stale cigarette smoke despite the NO SMOKING sign tacked to the wall.

Rivera motioned for me to sit down at one of the folding chairs that lined the table. Then the two officers disappeared, closing the door behind them.

I've seen this on TV, I thought. *They leave me here to sweat and get tense. They want to frighten me.*

About twenty minutes later, Rivera returned and took the chair opposite me. He wiped his mustache with his fingers, his dark eyes studying me. "Caitlyn, would you like some water? It's hot in here."

"That's okay," I said. "We won't be here for long, right?"

All I wanted to know was how much did they know? Did they bring me here to set a trap for me to confess? Were they going to arrest me?

"Yeah. Just a few questions," Rivera said, shifting his weight. He was too tall for the little chair.

"About Blade?" I said. I squeezed my hands together in my lap.

He nodded. He twirled a gold ring on the pinky finger of his left hand, twirled it slowly, his eyes locked on me. "We understand you were a friend of his."

"Well, we went out a few times," I said. "I didn't really know him. I think his family just moved here a few months ago."

I tried to return his stare. Somehow, I managed to keep my voice steady. I was glad there was no lie detector in the room.

A car horn honked somewhere outside. Rivera twisted the ring on his finger and kept his eyes on me. "Where were you Saturday night, Caitlyn? The night Blade was killed."

"Saturday night? I . . . uh . . . I was home," I said. "Remember? You and your partner came to my door? I told you then I hadn't gone out."

He let go of the ring and lowered both hands to the

edge of the table. Did he believe me? I couldn't tell any-thing by his blank expression.

"Try to remember," he said. "When was the last time you saw Blade?"

I hesitated. "I don't really remember. Maybe Thursday or Friday at Lefty's."

Rivera sighed again. He leaned across the table toward me. He rubbed the black stubble on one side of his face. "Caitlyn," he said, "why are you lying to me?"

26.

My whole body went cold. A choking sound escaped my throat. I struggled to breathe normally. "Wh-what do you mean?" I stammered.

Don't lose it, Caitlyn, I warned myself. *Don't let him mess you up. You can play this out.*

I tried to reassure myself. But my heart was going crazy like it was doing a drum solo, and Rivera's hard stare was sending chill after chill down my back.

"We have a witness," Rivera said, speaking softly, slowly.

Oh my God! Someone saw me kill Blade?

"We have a witness who told us you were one of the last people to see him alive."

I swallowed. I didn't say a word. I waited for him to continue.

He brushed a fly off his forehead. He rubbed his cheek again. "Caitlyn, is the witness telling the truth?"

"Yes," I said. "I guess. I'm sorry. I'm just so . . . so

upset. My brain isn't functioning. I mean, I've never had a friend die before."

I wiped sweat off my forehead. It had to be two hundred degrees in the tiny room.

"Well, do you want to tell me the truth now?" Rivera asked. "You were at the dance club called Fire Saturday night?"

"Yes. Yes, I was," I confessed, lowering my eyes. Then I snapped, "Who told you that?"

"Blade's girlfriend. Vanessa Blum," he replied.

Girlfriend? She said she was his girlfriend?

A sharp pain exploded in my chest. As if I had been stabbed.

Blade had a girlfriend. He was just playing with me.

"Okay. Yes," I said. "I went to the club." I crossed my arms tightly in front of me, trying to stop the pain, trying to shield myself from his questions.

But there was no escape. I had to tell the whole story. Or at least *part* of the story of Saturday night.

"I was supposed to go out with Blade," I said. "We had a date. But he stood me up at the last minute. So . . . I went to my friend Miranda's house for a while, and then I was bored. So I went to the dance club. You know. To see if any of my other friends were there." I took a breath.

"And you saw Blade?" Rivera urged me on.

I nodded. "Yes. I saw him there. And I was . . . well . . . shocked. I mean, we did have a date, and he told me he got hung up and couldn't make it. And then there he was, at Fire with another girl."

"And that made you angry?" Rivera demanded.

"Well . . ."

"You had a screaming fight with him at the bar?"

I felt totally trapped. How could I get out of this? Not by telling the truth. Could I get away with half-truths?

If only I knew how much Rivera knew.

"Yeah, sure. I was angry," I said. "He lied to me and there he was with this girl. Vanessa. So yes, I was angry. But . . . we didn't have a screaming fight."

Rivera's eyes widened. "You didn't?"

"No. No way," I said. "I told him off, and then I left the club."

This was all true. I was telling him the truth.

Rivera shifted his weight on the little folding chair again. His expression remained blank. "Then what?"

"Then I went home," I told him. "I was upset. I went up to my room. You came to my house, remember?"

"And found the front door open," he said. "Caitlyn, did you leave the door open? Were you so upset and angry that you left the front door open?"

"Maybe it was me," I admitted. "I don't know."

He toyed with the ring on his pinky finger again as he studied me. "So you went straight home from the club, and you didn't leave the house again Saturday night?"

I nodded. "I tried to go to sleep, but I couldn't."

Rivera took a long pause, as if he was trying to think of what to ask next. "You didn't go to his house and wait for him after you left the dance club?"

"No," I said. "I went home. I . . . I told you, we weren't that close. I was only at his house once. I'm not even sure I could find it."

Did Rivera believe me?

"Well, Caitlyn, how angry were you Saturday night? Would you say you were angry enough to get violent?"

"Of course not," I said. "I . . . I'm not a violent person. I've never had a real fight with anyone. I . . . think I was more hurt than angry. Just because he lied to me. You know."

Rivera nodded. He studied me for a long moment. Then he scooted his chair back till it hit the wall. He climbed to his feet. "I'm sorry if this was hard for you," he said. "I know—"

"Yes. Yes, it was hard," I said. I reached into my bag for a tissue and wiped my eyes. "I liked him. I really liked him. And now I'm totally freaked out knowing I was one of the last people to ever see him. And I'll never have a chance to make up with him. Never. I . . . can't stop thinking about it. I really can't." I wiped my eyes some more.

He opened the door and motioned for me to follow him out. "I appreciate your cooperation," he said. "Officer Miller will drive you back to the mall."

He waved to Miller, who had a desk against the wall

in the front room. I strode quickly toward the exit, eager to get away from there.

Rivera's voice followed me to the door: "Caitlyn, stick around, okay? I may want to talk to you again. "

27.

I hurried to the Cineplex, Diary. I was late but I didn't care. I needed to get back to a normal life, or at least go through the motions. I knew my life would never be normal again, never be like before.

I was edgy, alert to everything, so tense my skin prick-led. I knew the police would be back. I knew they'd be coming to arrest me any day. Arrest me for murdering Blade, and I had no way to prove I wasn't responsible. No way to prove that I was being controlled by Deena Fear.

Maybe, I could plead insanity.

Which was quite possible. I mean, my being insane.

Yes, I was insane for getting involved with Deena Fear. Insane for falling into her trap. Insane for going along with her scheme to bring poor dead Blade back.

Insane.

Was there any other word for it?

I hadn't heard from Deena since we had fled from the North Hills chapel. We had stared disbelieving into the empty coffin. Then we ran out the back door without saying a word to one another.

Deena ran to her car, expecting me to follow. But I took off down the street, running full-speed, the cool wind brushing my hot cheeks, the ground solid and real beneath my pounding shoes. I needed something real.

I needed to get away from her, away from the horror. My brain was exploding with questions. Had someone moved Blade's body earlier from its coffin? Perhaps refrigerated it or something to keep it in good shape? Had he been buried after all? Or had Deena brought him back to life the night before without realizing it?

That was truly crazy. But she said she'd been up all night preparing, doing whatever magic she did.

No. No. I refused to believe it.

For two days, I kept checking the local news websites. Waiting for the story of the missing body, the corpse stolen right out of the chapel. Every morning, I grabbed my dad's copy of the Shadyside *Citizen-Gazette* at breakfast and pawed through it, searching for the story.

But it wasn't there. It wasn't anywhere. And no one wrote about his funeral, either.

Dad looked up from his toaster waffles. "Since when are you interested in the news?"

"Uh . . . I thought my friend might be in it," I said.

He took the paper back and folded it to the sports section. He didn't ask why my friend might be in the news.

Dad doesn't like to talk in the morning until his second cup of coffee.

I didn't see Deena in school. I felt too distracted to be there. I couldn't listen to any of my teachers, and then Ms. Ryan, the gym teacher, called me away from our volleyball game and asked if I was feeling well.

I avoided Julie and Miranda. They wanted to be sympathetic and fawn over me and tell me they knew how bad I felt and how tragic the whole Blade thing was (if they only knew!) and ask what they could do to cheer me up.

Nothing. Nothing could cheer me up.

They were my best friends, and they meant well. I mean, they really did care about me. But I couldn't bear to eat lunch with them. While everyone marched to the lunchroom, I slipped outside.

A warm April day, more like summer than spring. I took a long walk behind the school, past the student parking lot, and the stadium.

Shadyside Park stretches behind the school. I sprawled on a bench, tilted my head into the sun, shut my eyes, and tried not to think. I thought of how you erase a whiteboard. Just wipe it clean, wipe everything away.

Start all over . . .

Of course, I couldn't do that. How could I wipe away all the horror that had come into my life?

I sat there in the sun, in the quiet park, daffodils popping through the ground, tiny new leaves unfurling on the still-wintry trees, half in a daze. I think I would have sat there all day. Except two women pushing baby strollers came ambling by, and one of the babies was crying.

The shrill sound snapped me out of my hazy daydreams. I jumped to my feet, shook myself like a dog, turned, and made my way back to school.

I searched for Deena Fear in the halls and waited for her by her locker after school. But she didn't appear.

I didn't really want to see her. I hoped I'd never have to see her again. But I needed to talk to her. I needed to find out if she knew anything. If she'd heard anything. If she knew why Blade's body wasn't in its coffin and why no one was reporting it missing and . . . and . . . ? My brain was spinning with so many questions. "Deena? Where *are* you?" I shouted to the empty hallway.

And now here I was. Making my way through the movie theater lobby. Back at work for the first time.

Of course, Ricky came running over as I stepped into the lobby. His face was filled with concern, his eyes wide, his mouth twisted in a pout of sympathy.

He grabbed both my hands in his. "Oh, Caitlyn, I'm so sorry. So sorry to hear about your friend."

"Thank you, Ricky," I muttered. I was waiting for him to let go of my hands.

"I know how you must feel," he said. "Losing someone you were close to so suddenly." He shook his head sadly. I thought he might start to cry.

I slid my hands out from his. "Thank you," I repeated. "I just thought . . . it would be better to get back to work."

He nodded. He had to squeeze my hands one more time. Then he turned and strode out of the lobby. *He was just being nice,* I thought. *But that was way icky.*

I washed my hands, then stepped behind the concession counter. The popcorn machine was getting low, so I added some oil and started it up. It was a busy afternoon. The theater had a special *Star Trek* double feature starting at five, and it drew a pretty big crowd.

I was wiping the counter down after the last customer had gone into the auditorium when my phone rang. I glanced at the screen. My friend Miranda.

I raised the phone to my ear. "Hey. How are you? I'm at work."

"I think you've been avoiding me," Miranda said. "I haven't talked to you in days."

"I . . . I've been weird," I admitted. "Sorry. It's been tough, Miranda. You know."

"Well, if you want to talk about it, I'm here," she replied. "I mean, if it would help at all."

"I don't know," I said. "I'm pretty messed up. I—"

"Julie and I want you to come to the basketball game at school tonight," she said. "Maybe it will help take your mind off things."

"I don't know. I think—"

"We could go to Alfonso's and share a pizza afterward," Miranda said. "Or maybe two. Like we used to."

I thought about it. I thought about how nice it was to have such considerate friends. Friends who were eager to help me.

"Well . . . maybe . . ." I said.

"It's going to be a good game," Miranda said. "We're playing Green Valley. I know you're not into basketball, but you should come, Caitlyn. We'll have fun."

"Well . . . okay," I said. "Okay. Thanks, Miranda. I'll meet you in the gym at seven thirty."

I clicked off. *Why not try to have some fun?* I thought. *It's just a basketball game.*

What could happen?

28.

There had been a tenth-grade dance in the gym on Saturday night, and some of the red-and-blue streamers were still hanging overhead. A few stray balloons lingered in one corner near the coach's office.

I was early. The game didn't start till eight. A few kids were already in the bleachers. They sat staring at their phones or talking with their friends.

I recognized some guys from my class up in the top row of seats, passing around bags of tortilla chips. I saw Michael Frost, a guy I went out with a couple of times last year. He was sitting with Lizzy Walker, a new girl in school.

Lizzy was a mystery girl. She arrived in the middle of senior year. No one knew anything about her. But the guys were interested in her because she was blonde and pretty and spoke with a sexy soft voice.

She was sitting with her leg pressed against Michael's, tossing her hair from side to side as she talked, her face close to his cheek. Even from this distance, I could see that Michael was entranced.

I was still staring at them when Julie and Miranda arrived. They both wore maroon-and-white Shadyside Tigers T-shirts pulled down over straight-legged jeans. They spotted me right away, hurried over, and we hugged.

"We're so glad," Julie said. "We didn't think you'd come."

"Sorry I've been such a downer," I said. "I just—"

Miranda clamped a hand over my mouth. "Don't talk about it. Seriously. Tonight is a fun night. Go, Tigers."

"Go, Tigers," I repeated, trying to show some enthusiasm.

Miranda sniffed my hair. "Mmmmm. Popcorn."

I rolled my eyes. "Tell me about it."

Julie guided me toward the bleachers. "Let's sit up high so we can see everything. Hey, maybe those guys will share their chips with us."

We started up the bleacher stairs. "No, wait." Miranda tugged me back. "You know I have a thing about heights. How about here? Right in the middle?"

We squeezed past Michael and Lizzy who sat pressed together on the aisle and dropped down on the bench in the middle of the row. On the court, both teams were practicing, taking jump shots from all over the floor, the balls bouncing everywhere, pounding the floor like drumbeats.

Green Valley is nearly fifty miles from Shadyside, so the

guest team bleachers across the floor were only about a third filled. Over the thunder of the balls, I could hear some kids from the other school chanting, "Giants! Giants! Giants! Go, Big Green!"

The team brought cheerleaders in their shiny, short green pleated skirts. And their mascot, a very tall, costumed character called the Jolly Green Giant. He did cartwheels along the front of the bleachers, and got a few of the Giants fans clapping and cheering.

I'm not into basketball. Actually, tennis is my sport. But it was great to be kidding around with Julie and Miranda and to be in the middle of a happy, cheering crowd.

The game started and the Giants quickly took an early lead. They had a couple of players who *had* to be eight feet tall. Well, maybe not. But they were a lot taller and *wider* than our players.

The Giants played a very aggressive game. A lot of shoving and elbows and charging into players. They had several fouls called against them, but they also bullied their way under the basket to score a lot of points.

Shadyside's shooting was off. They have two awesome three-point shooters. But tonight, the ball wasn't dropping for them.

Our team was down by twelve points, and I found myself really getting into the game. I was cheering and screaming, waving my fists, urging them on. Julie and Miranda kept glancing at me. I could see they were happy that I was enjoying myself.

And then the fun stopped.

I saw the two men in dark uniforms enter the gym.

I didn't recognize them until they strode closer, edging their way toward the bleachers along the sideline. The police officers. Rivera and Miller.

They walked slowly, stiffly, arms tensed at their sides. At their waists, I could see their holstered guns. They weren't paying any attention to the game. Their eyes were on the bleachers.

I knew why they were here. They had come for me. This was it. This was the end of my fun normal night. They had come to take me away.

I read it on their faces as they scanned the crowd. Row by row.

"Here I am." I had the urge to shout.

No way I could hide. No way they wouldn't see me.

Rivera's eyes stopped on me. A soft moan escaped my throat.

"Here I am. Here I am. The murderer. Here I am. Come and arrest me. Take me away."

29.

My whole body tensed as I watched the two cops at the bottom of the bleachers. The cheers of the crowd faded from my ears. All sounds faded away until I heard only the pulsing of my racing heartbeats.

Rivera turned and said something to his partner. Miller nodded. The two of them began to climb up the aisle.

They've seen me. They're coming for me.

I had a strong urge to open my mouth and scream, to let out all my horror, all my fear, and just scream and scream until I had no voice or breath left.

Somehow I held it in. I leaned forward on the bench, every muscle tensed, as I watched Rivera lead the way up the side of the bleachers.

He stopped three rows below me and pointed. Miller nodded. The two of them squeezed into the row and took seats about a third of the way across.

"Huh?" A startled gasp escaped my throat. I watched

the two cops settle themselves and turn to focus on the game.

Miranda turned to me. "What's wrong?"

"Uh . . . nothing. I . . . can't believe that last whistle. Johnson didn't foul that guy."

"Of course he did," Miranda said. "He practically took his head off."

Julie laughed. "Hey, you're really into this, Caitlyn."

I glanced at the backs of the two cops. "Yeah," I said. *Now that I can breathe again.*

I realized that I had to take my happy moments when I could. I knew it was only a matter of time before the police *did* come after me.

I gazed at the scoreboard. Only a minute left in the first half. Shadyside had pulled to within four points of the Giants. Kids were standing now, jumping up and down and cheering. Deafening excitement. The bleachers were actually rocking.

Julie, Miranda, and I jumped to our feet. A steal and a fast-break layup brought the Tigers within one basket. Someone called time out. I watched the players trot to their benches on the sidelines.

A flash of color caught my eyes. I peered across the gym to the visitors' bleachers.

I nearly fell over. I grabbed onto Julie and Miranda to catch my balance. A guy in a red hoodie hunched in the second row. He stood out among the green jackets and shirts of the visitors.

Of course, I thought of Blade. *No way* I could see a red hoodie and not think of him. I squinted into the glare of the bright gym lights, trying to see the guy more clearly. He had his head down and the hood pulled over his hair. I could see only the top of the red hood and his chest and arms.

My two friends didn't notice my alarm. They stood on both sides of me arguing about what kind of pizza to get after the game. Miranda liked to plan ahead. And she doesn't like pepperoni. We have this conversation nearly every time we go for pizza at Alfonso's.

I didn't join in. I was watching the boy in the red hoodie, waiting for him to raise his head. The buzzer rang, indicating the time-out was over.

The guy raised his head, and the hood fell back to his shoulders. I leaned forward, studying his face, his dark hair.

"Oh no."

Blade.

It *was* Blade!

He raised his eyes to the Shadyside bleachers. He was gazing right at me. The game started up. He didn't look away. He stared at me intensely from across the gym.

Before I could even think, I had shoved my way past Miranda and I was rushing to the aisle, stepping on feet, brushing kids back, everyone a blur, just a blur because I had the red hoodie in my eyes.

"Caitlyn? Hey—Caitlyn?"

"What's wrong? Where are you going?"

I heard my friends calling after me in alarm. I didn't turn back. I stumbled into the aisle, hurtled into a few kids blocking my way, and dove past some others.

I made it to the gym floor just as the half-time buzzer rang out. A groan went up from both bleachers. No one wanted the game to stop. My shoes slipped on a wet spot on the gym floor, and I nearly fell onto the team bench.

I took a deep breath and ran along the sidelines.

Blade is back.

I didn't ask any of the obvious questions. Had Deena Fear brought him back? Did he come back to haunt me? To accuse me? To let everyone know that I was his murderer?

I ran past the team bench where the players were grabbing towels and water bottles and heading to the locker room. I darted between two striped-shirt referees who were mopping their faces with towels, heatedly discussing some penalty call.

I ran against the crowd of kids coming down off the visitors' bleachers, making their way to buy hotdogs and drinks at the stand outside the gym.

"Blade! Hey, Blade!" I breathlessly shouted his name, my chest about to burst from running, from my shock. "Blade!"

My eyes ran along the bleachers. To the second row. Empty now. Empty.

No red hoodie. No Blade. He was gone.

I spun around, my eyes searching every face.

I'm not crazy. I didn't hallucinate him. He was here.

I felt a hard bump from behind. "Blade?"

I turned to see a big red-headed kid in a green-and-yellow Green Valley jersey. "Hey, sorry," he said. He had a large cup of Coke in each hand. "Didn't see you. Sorry."

"No worries," I said.

Then Julie and Miranda appeared beside me. "Caitlyn? What are you doing over here?" Julie demanded.

"You got up before halftime," Miranda said. "What's wrong?"

"I-I saw him," I stammered. "I saw Blade."

They both gasped. Julie wrapped an arm around my shoulders. "You mean someone who looks like Blade?"

"No." I stepped away from her. "Blade. I saw him. He was sitting right there." I pointed to the middle of the second row, now empty. "He . . . was staring at me. Staring across the gym right at me."

Miranda and Julie exchanged glances. They weren't prepared to deal with an insane person. They brought me here to snap me out of my depression, and now here I was, ruining everything.

Miranda shook her head, her face tight with concern. "Caitlyn, you know it couldn't be Blade. What made you think—"

"He was wearing the red hoodie," I said. "That's what made me look at him. The hood slipped off and . . . and . . ."

"Do you want to go home?" Julie asked. "Where's your car? I could drive you—"

"No!" I cried. "I have to find Blade. He's here. I'm not making it up, Julie."

I pictured Deena Fear. Pictured Blade's empty coffin once again. He was here. I knew he was here.

I broke away from them and ran toward the gym doors. I pushed through the double doors into the hall. Nearly knocked a girl over. "Sorry. Didn't see you."

My eyes searched up and down the hall. Several kids were lined up at the concession table. No. No sign of him. Their faces all blurred in front of me. No red hoodie. No Blade.

Back into the gym, the roar of voices ringing in my ears. The scoreboard buzzed. Almost time for the game to resume. The visitors' bleachers were filled, but no sign of Blade.

I waved to Julie and Miranda who were starting up the aisle of the home team bleachers. I cupped my hands around my mouth and shouted: "Hey, I have to go!"

No way I could stay. No way I could watch the game knowing that Blade was back, knowing that he saw me, stared at me from across the gym.

My two friends rushed back over to me. "You're going home?" Julie asked.

I nodded. "My car is in the student lot."

"I really think you should let us drive you," Julie said,

her eyes searching mine, as if trying to decide if I'd gone crazy or not.

"No. I'm fine," I said. "It's such a short drive. Really. I'm fine."

Miranda gave me a hug. She couldn't hide her distress. "We'll talk later," she said.

They turned to go back to their seats. I hurried from the gym, into the hall. Only a few stragglers out here. I heard the game start up, the drumbeat of the basketball on the floor, the roar of voices. The sounds followed me as I pushed open the back doors to the school and stepped into the night.

The air had turned cooler. The moon was hidden behind low clouds. I felt a few cold droplets of rain on my hair and forehead.

I turned toward the student parking lot, jammed with cars. The halogen lamps along the tall iron fence made the lot nearly as bright as day. Someone with a blue Toyota RAV4 had left the headlights on.

I saw my car halfway down the back row, facing out. And I saw the red hoodie.

Blade, leaning casually, his back against the driver's door of my car, waiting for me.

30.

I stopped and stared into the harsh halogen glare. Stared until the hoodie became a red glow in my eyes, and the rest of Blade vanished ghostlike behind the ray of red.

He pushed himself away from the car, standing up, his eyes on me. He didn't move toward me. Just waited there, still casual. Did he expect me to go running to him? To throw my arms around him and tell him how thrilled I was that he was back?

I forced my legs to move. Took a few steps toward him. And then the words tore from my mouth: "You can't be here. You're dead! You're dead, Blade. Why are you here?"

He gave a slow shrug. His greenish eyes glowed under the lights. He didn't say anything.

"Blade? What do you want? Why are you here? You know you can't be here." I couldn't stop myself. I knew I wasn't making any sense. I was talking to a dead person.

But he was there, leaning one hand on the side of my car. He was there. I wasn't imagining him.

"Blade—say something." My voice trembled on the air. Raindrops pattered the parking lot, the cars. "Did you come back to hurt me? What do you want? *Tell* me."

The wind ruffled his red hood. He didn't reply. He didn't move. He stood there. Waiting. Waiting for me to come closer.

And then what?

I had to get to my car. I had to get away from him. I didn't want to talk to a dead person. I didn't want to know why he waited for me there so silently, so patiently.

I wanted him to go away. And stay away.

Fear choked my throat. I brushed raindrops off my forehead.

I was only a few feet from him now. "Blade? What do you want?" I asked in a tiny voice. "Blade—please."

He didn't answer. He grabbed my wrist.

"Hey—let go!"

He pulled me close. He gripped both of my wrists and pulled me against him. His hands were hard and cold as ice.

"Let go! What are you doing? Let go!"

The blank green eyes glowed. He grabbed my face with both frozen hands. Spread his hands over the sides of my head and drew me to him.

He pressed his lips against mine in a hard kiss. An angry kiss. He held me there, held my face against his, pressed his lips, so hard and cold, against mine, grinding them against my lips until my mouth ached.

I finally pulled my head back, gasping for breath, the taste of his icy lips still on mine. And then I uttered a horrified gasp.

His lips were still sewn together.

I started to gag. I forced myself not to vomit. I rubbed my mouth but I couldn't get the cold of his lips off them.

He held my shoulders, breathing heavily into my face. His breath was rotten. It smelled like spoiled meat. Like death.

A twisted smile spread on the stitched-together lips. I could see the black thread clearly. Some of the stitches at one end had popped.

I struggled to back away, but he was too strong for me.

He slid both hands around my head and pulled me forward for another kiss. Choking, I struggled to breathe normally as he moved the cold dead lips over mine, caressing my cheeks with his thumbs as he held my head.

Held me in a kiss with a corpse. I thought it would never end.

The stitches scraped against my lips until I cried out in pain.

I stuck one leg behind his—and gave him a two-handed shove in the chest. He toppled backward and fell to the pavement. His eyes flashed with surprise.

I grabbed my car door and swung it open. I had the ignition key in my bag. I only had to push the *start* button to start the car. I dropped behind the wheel, tugged hard to close the door.

But Blade was on his feet. He grabbed the door by the handle and held it open. Grunting like an animal, his glassy green eyes gleaming, he reached for me with his other hand. Slapping at my shoulder, trying to get a grip on me.

He was grunting like a dog through his stitched-up lips, grunting and growling and grabbing at me. I struggled to shove him back. Then I grabbed the door handle with both hands and jerked it hard, pulled it with all my strength.

The door slammed on Blade's hand. He didn't even scream. Could he feel it?

One more hard pull and the door clicked shut. I pushed Start. The car revved up quickly. The chest of the red hoodie was pressed against my window. I ignored it. Slammed the car into Drive. Shot my foot down on the gas, and took off with a squealing roar.

I saw Blade tumble back. He sprawled over the hood of the car in the next space.

My car roared into the aisle. Too fast. Too fast. I had to brake hard to avoid crashing into the wire fence.

I was crazed. Heart beating like crazy. My head throbbing. My lips ached from those horrifying, sick kisses. I swung the car toward the exit. Nearly scraped the Rav4 with its headlights on at the end of the row.

And then I bumped out of the short driveway, onto Division Street. Made a wide right turn, forgetting to look for traffic. A horn honked angrily close behind me. I sped away. Sped through a stoplight. More horns honking.

I just had to move, had to get as far away from the living corpse as I could. Rain spattered the window, but I didn't turn on the wipers. I stared out through the shiny droplets, little diamonds sparkling against the dark night. Like driving through a dream.

Only this was a nightmare.

Somehow I made it home. I slammed on the brake in front of our garage. An inch or two from the garage door. The glare of the headlights off the wide white door filled the windshield with eerie white light.

I sat there staring into the light with my hands gripping the wheel. Sat there as if I didn't want to open the door and step back out into the world. My throat still tight. My lips scraped and burning.

I'm home.

Safe . . . for a while.

I cut the engine and started to reach for the headlights switch. But my hand stopped in midair.

What was that in my lap? Something sitting in my lap. What was it?

I reached down and picked it up. I raised it to my face to see what it was.

Blade's hand.

Blade's cold, dead hand. I'd sliced it off when I slammed the door.

I opened my mouth and started to scream.

PART
FOUR

31.

I tossed the hand into the alley behind my house. It made a sick soft *thud* as it bounced off a fence and hit the gravel.

Should I hide it under something? Should I bury it? I couldn't think straight. "No one ever goes back there," I told myself.

I couldn't breathe. My stomach churned. The hand felt hard and cold, curled into a fist. Sliced cleanly at the wrist, it didn't bleed at all.

It didn't bleed because Blade was *dead*.

I trembled in the light from the house that swept over the backyard. My eyes darted back and forth. Had Blade followed me? Had he come to take his hand back?

He won't leave me alone now. He'll want his hand and he'll want revenge.

I slipped into the house through the kitchen door. My parents had gone to bed, but they left a few lights on for me. I tiptoed silently up the stairs and to the bathroom across from my room.

I felt sick. My throat tightened. I leaned over the toilet and tried to throw up. But the waves of nausea faded.

I washed my face. I washed my lips. I could still taste those dead, hard lips on mine. I washed my hands three times.

I darted into my room and closed the door carefully behind me. I dropped onto the edge of my bed, clasping my hands together tensely in my lap.

I needed help, and there was only one person who could help me.

Deena Fear.

I wished I didn't need to see Deena again. I *never* wanted to see her. I pictured the man and woman in the glass cases. Were those really her parents? Did she really stuff them and put them on display there?

It couldn't be true. It *couldn't*. But I saw them there in that frightening room. And Deena actually bragged about it. Joked about using her taxidermy lessons on them.

I hugged myself to stop shivering. I suddenly realized I was *terrified* of Deena. Was she totally psycho? A crazed killer? I didn't want to go near her again.

But did I have a choice?

Even in my terror, I knew she was the only one who could help me.

Deena brought Blade back to life. She made me kill him. Then she brought him back.

Deena wanted him to be hers this time. But where was she? She was the only one who could control him. The only one who could protect me. My only hope was that she could stop him from coming after me.

"Deena." I whispered her name as I grabbed my phone. I pushed her number and raised the phone to my ear. It rang three times . . . four times. . . .

And then I heard a series of beeps. And a recorded woman's voice, much too loud, so loud I jerked the phone away from my ear, announced, "You have reached a number that has been disconnected. Please check the number and dial again."

Disconnected? No. No.

Why would Deena disconnect her phone?

I tried it again and got the same announcement. Then I clicked the phone off and tossed it in frustration, in anger, in fear, across my bed.

I'll find her in school tomorrow. She will know what to do about Blade. She will help me.

I tore off my clothes and tossed them in a heap in the middle of the floor. I pulled on a flannel nightshirt. It was a warm spring night, but I couldn't stop trembling.

The rain had picked up. It drummed against the window. My bed is right under the window. Normally, I love lying in bed, looking out at my backyard below.

But tonight, I pulled the covers up over my head. I shut my eyes tight and listened to the patter of the rain on the window glass.

Maybe the sound will soothe me to sleep, I told myself.

But, of course, that was crazy. I lay there curled under the covers until it got too warm to breathe. Then I tossed the covers off and tried sleeping on my side. I kept changing position, hoping to get the horrifying events of the night to fade to the background so I could catch some sleep.

But no. It all played over and over in my mind.

I suddenly remembered I had an oral report to give to the class tomorrow. "The History of the Stradivarius Violin." My grandfather was a classical violinist. He played with the Detroit Symphony and many other orchestras. He owned one of the priceless Stradivarius violins. He showed it to me when I was a little girl and explained why it was so valuable and perfect.

Shortly before my grandfather died, the violin was stolen. From all those years ago, I remember my grandmother saying that he died a few weeks later of a broken heart.

I was too young to fully understand then. But her words lingered in my mind. I wanted to add that personal story to my essay about Stradivarius violins. I knew Mr. Lovett, my English teacher, would appreciate it.

I'm a good writer, Diary. I love to write and tell stories. The essay was kind of special to me since my grandfather died when I was seven. I had started to write it. Actually, I had almost finished it.

What time was it? Two in the morning? Should I get up and work on it now? Maybe it would take my mind off Blade?

I yawned. No. No way I could concentrate. I didn't feel sleepy but I felt worn-out. Wrecked. Maybe if I tried to clear my mind. . . . Maybe count slowly down from one hundred to one. . . .

I was only down to ninety-three when I heard the rattling from outside my window. I sat up, alert.

The rain had stopped but the window glass was covered in raindrops. A bright half-moon floated high in the gray sky.

I listened. I heard another sound. Like a low cry. Maybe a cat?

I leaned forward and pressed my face to the glass and gazed down at the yard. "Oh no. Oh no."

I sucked in a breath as I saw Blade in his red hoodie.

He stood in the cone of yellow light that washed over the grass. The hood was down and I saw his green eyes gazing up at my window.

"No. Please." I shut my eyes and tried to erase him, tried to banish him, send him away. I wanted to plead with him, to beg him. *Disappear, Blade. You're dead. Please disappear.*

But when I opened my eyes, he hadn't moved. He stood in the light, red hoodie gleaming, and I saw the hand. The hand my car door had sliced off. He had it tucked in his hoodie pocket.

He found the hand. He had it.

I started to back away from the window, but he had already seen me. I watched him raise his good hand above his head.

What was he holding? What did he have clenched in his fist?

I squinted through the rain-smeared glass, struggling to focus. The light from the house caught the object in his fist. A knife. The blade flashed.

"Oh my God."

Blade held the knife above his head. Held it high so I could see it. His head tilted back. His eyes locked on mine.

I screamed as he plunged the knife down.

He sank the blade into his head and killed himself again.

32.

I swung my gaze to the bedroom door. Had Mom and Dad heard my scream?

Silence out in the hall.

I didn't want to look down into the yard again. I didn't want to see Blade sprawled on the grass with the knife buried in him.

But I had no choice. I had to know if he really was dead again. I had to know if—

Oh my God. No.

He didn't kill himself. He dug the knife into his mouth—and sliced the blade between his lips. He was using it to cut away the stitches, to free his mouth.

In the bright light, I could see the heavy black thread pop, see the stitches fall away until there were just a few scraps of black thread stuck to the sides of Blade's mouth.

Gripped in cold horror, my burning face against the cool window glass, I watched him test his mouth. Move his jaw up and down. His lips twitched. He slowly pulled them open. He slid his mouth up and down several times. He tugged bits of thread from his lips and worked his mouth some more.

Then he raised his eyes to me and shouted in a hoarse, ugly animal groan: "I'm back for you, Caitlyn. I'm back. I'll never leave you. Never!"

With a gasp, I slammed the shade down, stumbled back to my bed, and pulled the covers over my head.

I didn't want to go to school the next morning. How could I sit through classes with all this horror whirling in my brain? I started thinking up excuses to give my parents. But then I remembered I couldn't stay home. I had to go to school and find Deena Fear.

Deena was my only hope. From those old books in her family library, she had learned the secret, learned the power to bring Blade back to life.

She *had* to know a way to send him back to his coffin.

As I parked my car in the student lot, I thought once again about the two people frozen in glass cases at the back of Deena's house. I shuddered, my hands squeezing the steering wheel. A sensible person would stay as far away from Deena as she could.

But I wasn't a sensible person. I was a crazed, terrified person. Every sound, every fast movement of color or light, made me jump. Every burst of red made me want to scream. I knew I'd see that red hoodie forever in my nightmares.

Did Blade really say he would stay with me forever? I had to take his words seriously. I had to believe he meant it. Even though just thinking about it made my stomach churn and my heart start to do flip-flops in my chest.

Deena, where are you?

I waited in the front hall until it was almost time for the bell to ring. She didn't show.

I asked some kids if they knew which homeroom Deena was in. No one seemed to know. With her strange, dark looks, her wild tangles of black hair all the way down her back, and her black outfits and her general weirdness, kids stayed away from her.

She was a total loner. I don't know if she had any friends at all in school. She wasn't in any of my classes. I never saw her with anyone.

The bell rang. The hall had emptied out. Everyone was in homeroom. I peeked into a few rooms on my way to Ms. Chow's room. I didn't see her.

Ms. Chow looked up from her laptop as I walked in. "Please close the door, Caitlyn," she said. "Try to be a little more prompt, okay?"

I closed the door behind me. "Ms. Chow, do you know what homeroom Deena Fear is in?" I asked.

She squinted at me. She scratched her straight black hair, which she wears very short with straight bangs across her forehead. "Deena Fear? I'm sorry. I don't know her, Caitlyn. Is there a problem?"

"Well . . ." I hesitated. I saw Julie at the end of the front row, watching me, her face tight with concern. "It's kind of an emergency," I said. "I really need to find her."

Ms. Chow nodded. "Why don't you go to the office? Mrs. Vail can tell you where to find her."

"Thanks." I dropped my backpack onto my desk. "I'll be right back. I really appreciate it, Ms. Chow."

"Hey, Caitlyn," Julie called to me from across the classroom.

But I was already out the door and into the hall. Silent and empty out here. The two gym teachers were having some kind of conference in front of the trophy display case. They nodded at me as I jogged past them.

The principal's office is near the front entrance. I stepped inside. A couple of solemn-looking boys sat hunched on the bench in front of the main desk. Sophomores, I think. Must have been in some kind of trouble.

Mrs. Vail, the office secretary, had a phone pressed to her ear. She stood at the desk, sifting through papers as she talked. I stepped up to the desk and rested my arms on the desktop in front of her.

She nodded and kept on talking. It seemed to be something about the hot-lunch program. She kept saying, "I have no control over that. The state tells us what to serve."

I was practically bursting, silently begging her to get off the phone. If she talked much longer, homeroom would be over and I'd be late for Advanced English and my violin report.

I let out a long whoosh of air when she finally hung up. "Caitlyn, what can I do for you?"

"I need to find Deena Fear," I said. "It's kind of important. Can you tell me her homeroom?"

"That's an easy one," she said, smiling at me. "I like the easy requests."

She moved to the desktop computer at the edge of the counter and began to type rapidly on the keyboard. "I'll just pull up her schedule. What was her name again?"

I told her.

Mrs. Vail turned her gaze on me. "A Fear? From the famous Fear family? Really? How come I don't know her?"

I shrugged.

She returned to the computer, squinting at the screen. "That's strange," she murmured. She typed some more. "D-e-e-n-a, right?" She spelled the name.

"Right," I said. I leaned over the counter, trying to read the screen over her shoulder.

Mrs. Vail rubbed her chin. "Let me bring up the student directory. Is she a senior like you?"

"Yes. I'm pretty sure she's a senior."

"Okay. No problem." She typed some more. Then she studied the screen. She scrolled up and down the list of students.

"Is she new?"

"No. I don't think so. I don't really know."

She typed some more. Gazed at the screen intently.

Then she turned to me. "Caitlyn, there must be some mistake. There *is* no student named Deena Fear enrolled at our school."

33.

I tried to hide my shock, but I guess I didn't do a very good job. Mrs. Vail squeezed my hand. "Caitlyn? Are you okay?"

No. I'm not okay. I'm losing my mind. I'm inventing imaginary people.

I swallowed hard. My throat suddenly felt dry as sand. It took me a few seconds to assure myself that I didn't invent Deena Fear.

She was definitely real. Julie and Miranda had both seen her and talked about her that night when I bumped into her at Lefty's.

"She's real," I murmured. I didn't realize I was talking out loud.

"Maybe she goes to Collegiate," Mrs. Vail offered. That's the private girls' school in North Hills. "Have you seen her here in school?"

I wanted to get away from Mrs. Vail. She was gazing at me so suspiciously, like maybe there was something wrong with me. She is a nice person, but you don't want to confide in her. Anything you tell her she goes and tells to Mr. Hernandez, the principal.

"Actually . . ." I said. I tilted my head, thinking hard. "I guess I've only seen her out of school." I forced a smile. "Thanks, Mrs. Vail."

I didn't give her a chance to reply. I spun away and bolted from the office, nearly knocking over the two gym teachers, who were walking in.

The hall was bustling now, crowded and noisy. Homeroom had ended and everyone was heading to their first period class.

I moved slowly to my English class. Some kids called out to me, but I ignored them. I kept rubbing my forehead, massaging my temples as I walked. My head felt about to explode.

This was an Advanced English course, mainly for creative writing students. We all sit around a big, round table and share our stories and essays and critique them.

Normally, this is my favorite class. But now, I just wanted to hide in a corner, shut my eyes, and try to think. Of course, that was impossible. There's nowhere to hide at a round table.

And naturally, Mr. Lovett tapped me on the shoulder as I walked to my seat and said, "You'll go first this morning, Caitlyn."

As the other kids settled in, I pulled my essay from my bag. I don't get nervous reading in front of the whole class.

I'm pretty confident as a writer, and, everyone knows I'm not shy.

But today, my hands were shaking as I glanced through the pages I had written. The essay wasn't quite finished, and I wished I had time to polish it. My head was still throbbing. I hoped maybe reading the essay to everyone would give me a chance to calm down and stop puzzling over Deena Fear.

That didn't happen.

When Mr. Lovett gave the signal, I stood up and introduced my essay. "It's about the Stradivarius violin," I said. "I wrote it because this priceless instrument has special meaning to my family."

Mr. Lovett leaned forward and crossed his hands on the table. "Interesting," he murmured. "Go ahead, Caitlyn."

I started to read. "Stradivarius musical instruments were made in the seventeenth and eighteenth century by an Italian family named Stradivari. Today, they are valuable beyond belief, not just because of the quality of the workmanship, but because only 650 of them survive in the entire world."

I raised my eyes from the paper to see if everyone was listening. And uttered a gasp when I saw Blade. He stood in the open doorway.

He wore his red hoodie. One sleeve was pulled down low, covering the stump where his hand was missing. His hair was disheveled, falling around his pale white face.

He gave a thin smile as our eyes met. His eyes flashed.

Then he raised the back of his hand to his lips. He puckered his dead lips and, eyes locked on me, began to make loud kissing noises against his hand.

I lowered the essay and pointed to the door. "Don't you hear that?" I cried. "Don't you hear what he's doing? Look! See him? Do you see him there? It's Blade!"

Chairs scraped as everyone turned to the door.

But Blade was gone. The doorway was empty.

They quickly turned back to gape at me. I heard whispers and some muffled laughter.

"Caitlyn, I don't see anyone."

"What are you talking about?"

"Blade? You mean the kid who was killed?"

I tossed my essay onto the table, shoved my chair out of the way, and ran. I hurtled out of the classroom. Mr. Lovett's startled shouts followed me down the hall.

I lowered my shoulder and pushed open the side door to the school. I burst outside, breathing hard, my temples throbbing.

"I can't go back there," I told myself. "I can't go anywhere. Not till Blade is gone. But . . . how do I get rid of him?"

34.

I knew Deena Fear was the only one who could answer that question. I jogged into the student parking lot. I glanced in all directions.

Every nerve in my body was tense. My skin prickled. I felt sure that Blade would come leaping out at me.

The parking lot was deserted. Everyone was in class. Across the street, I saw a woman pushing a baby stroller. A tall white poodle followed after them. Normal life.

I wanted my life to be normal, too.

I climbed into my car. The steering wheel was hot from the sun burning through the windshield. I pulled out of the narrow parking place.

I glimpsed someone watching me from the school entrance. Was it Mr. Lovett? I didn't care. How could I care about school? How could I care about anything with a living corpse following me, haunting me?

The drive to Deena's house was a blur of flashing lights and streams of sunlight, shade then sun, houses sliding past, trees and cars and everything . . . everything just a jumble, a pulsing wave of motion and color. I didn't even realize I had turned onto Fear Street until the street became dark under the archway of tangled old trees.

As I reached the cul-de-sac where the street ends and the woods begin, Deena's house came into view. No car parked in front.

A black cat sat watching me from the front yard, very still, green eyes glowing, half-hidden in the tall weeds that led up to the house. The green eyes reminded me of Blade. And once again, I saw those glassy blank eyes green as emeralds, pictured them watching me as he stood in the classroom doorway making those obnoxious sounds. Enjoying himself. Having fun as he haunted me and drove me crazy.

I pulled to the curb and climbed out of the car, my eyes on the house. Sunlight reflected off the windows along the front. I couldn't see inside them.

The cat didn't move. It sat up straight as if ready to defend its territory. Its eyes followed me as I made my way past it to the door at the side of the house.

I pushed the doorbell. I didn't hear it ring inside. I waited a short while. The cat lost interest and wandered toward the burned-out remains of the Fear Mansion.

I could feel my heartbeats start to race. I rang the bell again. Then I knocked on the door. "Deena? Are you home? Deena?"

Silence.

The morning sun, now high in the sky, beamed down hard, but it didn't warm me. A chill covered my body, as if I'd just stepped from a cold bath.

"Deena? Where are you?"

I pulled out my phone. I studied her number again. I'd called it before today, and it had worked. Maybe if I tried it again . . .

I punched it and waited. *Please be there. Please answer.*

No. I got the same message telling me the number had been disconnected. With a sigh, I dropped the phone into my bag. I turned and pounded the door with both fists. Pounded until my knuckles throbbed.

"Deena? Deena?" I was about to totally lose it. I could feel myself about to snap, about to explode into a million pieces. "Deena?"

A window slid open at the side of the house. A head poked out. I squinted into the glare of the sun and recognized Deena. "You're home?" I said in a tiny, choked voice.

"Caitlyn, it's you," she said. "I've been expecting you."

Expecting me?

The window slid shut. A few seconds later, I heard footsteps inside the house, the front door swung open. "I rang and knocked," I said breathlessly. "I've been shouting your name and—"

She motioned for me to step inside. "I was in the back. Getting ready," she said. "Getting ready for you."

I edged past her into the small front entryway. The

house smelled strange, as if something was burning. "Do you have something on the stove?"

She shook her head. "No. But I *am* cooking something up."

I didn't like the sound of that. I tried to interpret the thin smile that spread on her black lipsticked lips, but I couldn't figure it out. Was she making a joke?

She had her long hair tied back with a wide purple ribbon, but strands had come loose and fell about her owlish face. She wore a satiny purple top over black straight-legged jeans.

She took a few steps toward me. I instinctively stepped back.

"I . . . looked for you in school," I blurted out.

"But, Caitlyn, I don't go to your school."

"I didn't realize," I said. "Where do you go?"

"Actually, I'm homeschooled." For some reason, that made her laugh. A scornful laugh.

"By your parents? You said your parents are dead," I said.

She laughed again. "I homeschool myself."

I nodded. My fists were clenched. Every muscle in my body was tensed. *Was I crazy to come here?*

No. Just desperate.

She studied me. She seemed very amused. "Why are you stalling? We don't have to chat like we're best friends. I know why you came."

"Okay," I said. "Can you . . . can you help me?"

Her smile faded. "I think I can. I'm very prepared. I have what we need."

I shook my head. "Deena, you're talking in mysteries. What are you saying?"

She reached under the oversized purple blouse. She pulled something out from beneath her shirt, something round, a little smaller than a softball.

A hand. Coiled into a fist.

Blade's hand.

I stared at it. The thumb poking over the curled fingers. The hand had turned a light purple color. "H-How . . . did you get that?" I stammered.

"Never mind," Deena said. "It doesn't matter." She tossed the hand up, then caught it in her palm. Tossed it again and caught it. Then she motioned me toward the hall. "Caitlyn, are you ready to rock and roll?"

35.

Deena led me down the long, shadowy hall to her room. The burning smell grew stronger as we walked. And as I followed her into the room, I saw that it came from dozens of burning candles, black candles that she had placed on every surface.

Eleven tall black candles formed a pentagram on the floor. The candles were scented and filled the air with a tangy incense aroma, kind of cinnamon.

The parrot made a chirping cry as I came near and flapped its wings as if it wanted to escape its perch. Three or four silvery fish floated through the aquarium on the table to the right of the parrot's perch.

Deena didn't speak, silently tossed Blade's hand up and down as we walked to the center of the room. Red morning sunlight filled the glass wall looking out on the Fear Street Woods.

She motioned to two black, square cushions she had set down in the middle of the tall, burning candles on the floor. "You sit there, Caitlyn," she said, breaking the silence.

I hesitated. "Wh–what are we going to do?"

"You'll see. We have a lot of work to do."

She walked to the table and picked something up from beside the aquarium. I recognized it as she draped the chain around her neck. The silver bird amulet. She arranged it over her purple blouse and returned to the pentagram.

She carefully stepped between the flames and, without warning, tossed the hand to me.

I fumbled it. Caught it before it hit the floor. "You hold it," Deena said, taking her seat across from me, so close our knees almost touched.

I gripped Blade's hand in both hands, afraid I would drop it. The hand had hardened. It felt like grainy plaster. The thumb and fingers were locked tight. At the stub end where the wrist had been, I could see dark spots where there once were veins.

I shuddered. How did I get involved with this terrifying girl?

"Deena, tell me," I insisted. "What are we doing here?"

She squinted at me through her big, round glasses. "Bringing Blade here, of course." She raised the amulet off her chest with one hand and smoothed the front of it with two fingers.

"Bringing him here?"

She nodded. Candlelight flickered off her pale face, reflected in her glasses. "He betrayed us again," she murmured. "Well . . . actually, he betrayed *me*."

Blade's hand felt heavy between mine. I didn't want to hold it. I lowered it to my side to get it out of sight. A wave of nausea rolled up from the pit of my stomach.

"Betrayed you? He's been haunting *me*," I said. "He said he would never leave me."

Her black lips tightened into an angry scowl. "That's exactly my point, Caitlyn. It was supposed to be *my* turn. I worked all that night to bring him back . . . to bring him back to *me*, not to you."

She tossed the loose strands of hair off her face. "He betrayed me again. I cannot allow it."

Suddenly, without thinking, my most frightening thought burst from my lips. I never should have said it. But it was there in my mind, terrifying me as I sat cross-legged across from her. As I sat there, such an easy victim.

"Deena, if you killed me . . . Blade might be yours. Is that your plan? To get me out of the way?"

Her eyes widened in shock and she uttered a short gasp. "Kill you? Of *course* not. What are you *thinking*? You're my best friend in the world."

She's crazy. Totally insanely psycho.

I swallowed, trying to force down my nausea. "So you're going to bring Blade here and—?"

"Explain to him," she said. She leaned over a black candle, lowering her face to the flame. She raised the amulet in front of her. "Caitlyn, pick up Blade's hand. Hold it in front of you. We want him to know we have it."

Obediently, I cupped the hard purple hand between my trembling hands. I raised it high.

"He will come," Deena said, lowering her voice to a whisper. "He will know we have it, and he will come for it. And then . . ." She raised her eyes to me. ". . . We will have him."

She dropped her gaze to the amulet and lowered it to the candle flame. Shutting her eyes, she began to chant. Words in a strange language I'd never heard.

Her lips moved quickly, her tongue clicking against her teeth, her eyes shut, the sound of her voice just a murmur against the flickering light, a whisper so light, I wasn't sure I was hearing it.

She didn't move a muscle. Kept the amulet in place over the flame and whispered her strange words, her back straight, her legs spread out from the cushion.

I held the hand in front of me. My arms started to ache, and my back stiffened. I shifted my weight but it didn't help. I took deep breaths and wondered how long Deena would chant, how long it would take before Blade came knocking on the door.

And then what? Then what? Deena was being so mysterious. She didn't want me to know her entire plan.

Was she keeping it a secret because it would end badly for me, too?

I didn't buy that BFF nonsense. I knew I was in danger, too.

But I couldn't just jump up and run. If she really wanted to help me get rid of Blade . . . If she really wanted to use her powers to send Blade back to his coffin . . . I had to stay. I had to do what she asked.

I shifted my weight again. My arms throbbed. My back ached. I stared straight ahead at Deena and listened to her drone on . . . and on.

My eyelids suddenly felt heavy. The soft rush of her whispered words were lulling me to sleep. I struggled to stay alert—and gasped when something moved between my hands.

I gazed down and saw the fingers on Blade's hand start to move.

I let out a horrified cry and dropped the hand to the floor in front of me. It made a squishy *thud,* bounced once, and stopped at Deena's ankles. And I stared in horror as the dead fingers slowly unfurled. The thumb slid out stiffly, and the fingers curled and uncurled, as if testing themselves.

Deena opened her eyes for only a second. She glimpsed the moving hand, like a fat purple insect trying to get off its back. Her expression didn't change. She closed her eyes again. She chanted softly.

Gripped in horror, I watched the hand flop onto its other side. Like a crab, it began to crawl over the floor.

"Deena—" I shouted. "It's moving. It's crawling away." I couldn't hold in my terror.

"That means Blade is near," she said, still whispering. "That means he is coming. Listen. Listen for his knock, Caitlyn."

Fingers scrabbling steadily across the floor, the hand crawled toward the table. The parrot squawked and shuffled its wings, its eye on the approaching creature.

"Blade is near," Deena whispered. "Listen carefully. Listen for his knock."

I realized I'd been holding my breath. I let it out in a long *whoosh*.

I froze again when I heard a sound. A soft *thump*.

Where was it coming from?

Deena stopped her chant and tilted her head, listening.

Thump . . . Thump . . .

Someone knocking softly on the glass wall.

"He's here," Deena whispered.

Thump . . . Thump . . .

36.

I froze as chill after chill rolled down my back. I couldn't
breathe. I couldn't move. Finally, I forced myself to
turn to the glass wall.

Thump . . . Thump . . .

I shielded my eyes with one hand against the harsh sunlight. Then I uttered an astonished cry and jumped to my
feet.

Deena and I both stared at the black cat up on its
haunches. It peered into the room from the other side of
the glass and tapped the wall with one paw.

Thump . . . Thump.

Not Blade. Not Blade.

Deena let out a long sigh. Her breath blew out one of
the candles. It sizzled and sent up a thin column of black
smoke.

Her shoulders drooped. She tossed the amulet onto one
of the cushions. "It didn't work, Caitlyn," she murmured,
avoiding my eyes. "Blade is out of my power."

Thump. The cat tried one more knock. Then it lowered itself to all fours and took off, its tail raised high, sprinting through the tall weeds of the backyard.

Once again, I felt cold all over. Strange how fear can control your body temperature. Fear and shock. I really expected to see Blade in the glass. Now that he wasn't there, I didn't know what to say or what to do next.

Deena picked up the hand, which was halfway to the aquarium table. The fingers curled as she lifted the hand off the floor. She tossed it into the aquarium. The water splashed violently and the fish inside scattered. The hand sank to the bottom and didn't move.

I stood there with my mouth open, trying to clear my head. I was surprised to see that Deena had tears running down her face. "All my energy," she murmured. "I used it all. I'm drained, see. The dead take so much energy. To bring them . . . and to send them back again. I . . . I don't have it, Caitlyn. I'm drained."

"But, Deena—" I started.

She wiped her tears with her fingers. Her eyes were narrow slits. Her cheeks were pale and puffy. The color had faded from her lips. "Drained. The amulet is empty. My words have no power."

She grabbed my shoulder. Her hand was ice cold. "I can't help you, Caitlyn. Blade is out there and he's on his own." She sighed. "I guess I took on too much. I thought I knew how to bring him here, how to control him. My family has always had such strong powers. But . . . I wasn't ready."

"Deena, that doesn't help me," I cried, backing away from her grip on my shoulder. "He's following me everywhere. He's haunting me and he says he'll never leave."

She shook her head wearily. "What can I say? I tried."

"But I can't live like this!" I screamed. "I can't live with a dead boy following me everywhere, grabbing me, kissing me with his dead lips, fighting, haunting me. How can I live with that?"

"Caitlyn, listen to me. I'm telling you the truth. I can't do anything," she said. She leaned against the wall. Her face grew even paler. In the harsh sunlight through the glass wall, she nearly disappeared. "You have to deal with Blade on your own."

"Huh?" I gasped. "On my own? What on earth do you mean, Deena? What can I do?"

"Isn't the answer obvious?" she said. "You have to kill him again."

37.

At my shift behind the popcorn counter that afternoon, I must have looked dazed or distracted. Ricky kept coming over and asking if I was okay. "If you'd like, you can take a ten-minute break," he said after I'd been on duty for only an hour. What a guy.

The theater was pretty crowded. I kept my eyes on the lobby entrance. Anyone wearing red made my breath stop. I knew Blade would show up. I knew he'd come to haunt me, to terrify me.

By the end of my shift, the tension from waiting and watching for him made me feel exhausted. Ruined. I almost forgot I'd made a plan to meet Julie after work.

I met her at Fresh Chopped, the salad restaurant in the mall near the Cineplex. We meet there a lot since Julie is a vegetarian. "How's it going?" she asked, her eyes studying me.

I shrugged. "Not bad. Do I smell like popcorn?"

She nodded.

We made our salads. I didn't pay much attention to what I put in mine. My stomach felt too tight to be hungry.

We slid across from each other in a booth away from the open double doors. In the next booth, two little kids were whining and complaining to their mother.

"But I *hate* salad."

"The lettuce gets stuck in my teeth. I *hate* this. It's yuck."

"We want McDonald's!"

"It's delicious," the mother argued. "Eat some of it and I'll buy you some ice cream."

"With sprinkles?"

"Okay. With sprinkles."

That seemed to quiet them down. Bribery almost always works with little kids.

Julie mixed the dressing into her salad with a fork. Her dark eyes were still on me. Her straw-blonde hair fell loosely to the shoulders of her striped tank top.

I noticed a bandage over her right earlobe. I pointed. "What happened to your ear?"

She rolled her eyes. "A piercing accident."

"You got your ears pierced again? That's very bold of you." As I've said, Diary, Julie is usually timid about things. She says she's "old-school."

"Yes. I wanted two holes. But the guy messed up or something. It got infected."

I tsk-tsked.

Julie stirred her salad some more. "Let's not talk about me," she said. "You left school this morning. What's up with that?"

I set my fork down. "Why? Were people talking about me?"

"Caitlyn, I *saw* you leave. You ran out the door like you were being chased. Were you sick or something?"

I opened my mouth to answer, then stopped, my brain spinning. And in that instant, with Julie peering across the table at me with such concern, I decided to tell her the truth.

I had to confide in someone. Deena Fear admitted she could be no help. But I couldn't face this entirely on my own.

"Julie," I started. "I know this is going to sound totally crazy, but I'm going to tell you the truth. Please listen to me. Please believe me, no matter how nuts it sounds."

She squeezed my hand. "Are you in trouble, Caitlyn?"

"No," I said. "I mean . . . yes. I mean . . ."

"Take a breath, okay. You're scaring me," she said. "Take a breath and start at the beginning. You know you can trust me, right?"

I nodded. I leaned over the table so I could whisper. I didn't want my story to scare the little kids in the booth behind me.

"Blade is back," I whispered. "Remember? They didn't bury him? Deena Fear brought him back from the dead. She—"

"You've been hanging out with Deena Fear?" Julie said, narrowing her eyes at me.

"Not hanging out exactly," I replied. "But she has powers. You know her family's story. They're all weird and they . . . can do things. And she brought Blade back to life. And . . ."

"Caitlyn, you're hyperventilating," Julie interrupted. "You're scaring me. Try to calm down."

Behind me, the two kids were arguing about where to go for ice cream. They both wanted Dairy Queen. Their mother was insisting on Tastee-Freez.

A wave of sadness washed over me. I wished I could talk about normal happy things like ice cream.

"Blade is back from the dead, Julie," I whispered. "And he came back to haunt me, to torture me, to terrify me."

Julie shook her head hard. She swept her blonde hair back. "Why, Caitlyn? Why you?"

I hesitated. *Should I tell her the whole story?*

Yes, I decided. It was all spilling out of me. I couldn't hold it in any longer.

"He's haunting me because I killed him, Julie. I'm the one. I'm the one who stabbed him. And now . . . now he's come back for revenge."

I grabbed both of her hands on the tabletop. "Do you believe me? *Please* say that you believe me. Please, Julie."

She stared at me for a long moment. I could practically see the gears of her brain spinning. She didn't move. She didn't blink.

Finally, she nodded. "I believe you, Caitlyn. I believe you."

I squeezed her hands. I wanted to jump up and hug her. "Oh, thank you!" I cried. "I can't tell you how much that means to me, Julie. I can't tell you how much better I feel that you know the truth now."

"You must be so frightened, Caitlyn," she said. "Blade back from the dead? It's like a horror movie. What are you going to do about him? What *can* you do? You have to get rid of him. You have to—"

"Deena Fear tried to help, but she couldn't," I said, my voice breaking. "I-I don't know what to do next. I'm so scared. I'm scared all the time." I held my breath, trying to hold back my tears. "I'm just so glad to have someone who believes me."

"We've been friends since sixth grade," Julie said. "I want to help you. Maybe I can help you."

"Help? How?" I asked. I watched a group of guys from our school walk into the restaurant. One of them was wearing a red sweatshirt. It made me gasp. Then I realized it was actually a maroon-and-white Shadyside High sweatshirt.

"Come to my house," Julie said. She slid out of the booth. "In half an hour, okay? Come in half an hour. Maybe I'll be able to help you. I mean, maybe."

"Okay," I said. "Okay. Half an hour. I'll kill some time here in the mall. I'll be there. Thanks, Julie. I mean, really. Thanks."

I watched her hurry away. Neither one of us had touched our salads. But I felt so much better, knowing that I had a true friend who believed me, believed my story no matter how insane it sounded.

How did she think she could help me? I didn't have a clue. But I was no longer alone.

I made my way to the exit. One of the guys from school called to me. I waved, but I didn't go over to them.

I wandered around the mall, just gazing into windows, not really seeing anything. The place was nearly empty. A lot of tables were filled at the food court in the basement. But bored salespeople stood around in empty stores, leaning on counters, their eyes on the clock, waiting for nine so they could close.

I remembered I had to buy a birthday present for my dad. I saw a Brooks Brothers store across the aisle. I took a few steps toward it, then stopped. I was in no mood to shop for anything.

I glanced at my phone. Time to head to Julie's house. My car was in the lot at the other end, near the Cineplex. I walked quickly past the stores, not seeing anything now but a blur of color and light.

My car stood all by itself in Row B. I felt a chill tighten the back of my neck. Parking garages give me the creeps. I thought about the guy who tried to rob me after work that night. You're just so totally vulnerable in a deserted parking garage.

My car squealed around a turn as I followed the circling aisle down toward the exit.

Julie lives on Bank Street, a short drive from the mall. She has two younger sisters, so there are five in her family. Their house is small, almost like a cottage. The kitchen, dining room, and living room are all one open room. Julie's sisters share a bedroom.

Julie says she doesn't mind being a little cramped. Her main complaint about the house is that it has only one bathroom. When her sisters go in to do their hair, it can take hours!

She says she loves her family because they're all pretty mellow. Bathroom time is the only thing they fight about. I know they were thinking of moving to a bigger house before Mr. Nello hurt his back. He was an assistant manager at a Walmart warehouse, but he had a bad accident unloading a truck. Now he gets some kind of disability.

I had all these thoughts about them as I drove. I guess I was trying to think about normal things, trying to keep my mind off my terrifying troubles. A few minutes later, I parked my car at the curb and walked up their small, square front yard. Her sister's scooters leaned against the front stoop. A jump rope was tangled around a low evergreen shrub at the foot of the steps.

I took a long breath of the cool night air and held it for just a second. Then I climbed onto the narrow stoop and rang the doorbell.

The door swung open almost instantly. Julie greeted me with a solemn face. "Hi, Caitlyn. Come in."

I stepped into the small front room. Saw the people standing there, standing there so stiffly. And I let out a cry: "What are *you* doing here?"

38.

D iary, I was trapped.

My mom stood behind Julie, her eyes moist, her chin trembling the way it always does when she's upset. Dad stood beside her, one hand on her trembling shoulder. He squinted at me as if he didn't recognize me.

"Come in," Mom said. "Come sit down, Caitlyn." She spoke slowly, softly as if she was speaking to a sick person.

I saw Julie's parents huddled together behind the couch at the back of the room. Julie's cheeks were bright pink. She could see the anger on my face, the betrayal I felt.

"I had to call them, Caitlyn," she said, clasping her hands tensely in front of her. "I had no choice."

"Why?" I said coldly. My jaw was clenched. "Why did you think you had to ambush me?"

"No one is ambushing anyone," Mom said.

"What was I supposed to do?" Julie asked, near tears. "What you were saying . . . What you were telling me at that restaurant was so crazy . . . ? I was worried about you.

I mean, really worried. You need help, Caitlyn. I mean . . ." Her voice trailed off.

Mom took my hand and squeezed it between both of hers. "We came as soon as we could. Julie said you were having a breakdown."

A breakdown?

She wouldn't let go of my hands. Her watery eyes peered into mine. Dad took my arm and pulled me to the couch. "Sit down. Come sit down. You're not well. I can tell by your eyes."

"Thanks, Doctor," I said sarcastically.

"Can I get anyone any coffee or tea?" Mrs. Nello chimed in.

No one answered her.

I could hear Julie's sisters talking upstairs in their room. I had a strong impulse to break away from my parents, run up there and join them.

"We're so sorry to intrude," my mom told Julie's mom.

"You're not intruding. I completely understand. If there's anything I can do. . . ."

"Caitlyn, I'm sorry." Julie was still apologizing. She stood by the front door, as if she was afraid to come near me. "You're my friend," she said. "I couldn't bear to see you in trouble. Please—forgive me."

"Nothing to forgive," My dad answered for me. He sat down next to me on the couch. He kept some distance between us, like I was contagious or maybe a wild animal that might attack him if he got too close.

Mom stood over me, her arms crossed in front of her. "Tell us what you told Julie. Okay, Caitlyn? Tell us the story so we can help you. Don't be afraid."

"You don't understand!" I screamed. "You don't understand! It isn't a story. I didn't tell Julie a *story*! You don't understand!"

I was shrieking at the top of my lungs. I realized I truly *did* sound like a crazy person.

"Screaming won't help," Dad said softly.

"This isn't going to help, either," I said sharply.

"Let's have a talk," Mom said. She motioned for me to slide over so she could sit on my other side. "That's what families do, Caitlyn. They help each other."

She and Dad were talking to me like I was a mental patient, and they both had these wet-eyed stares that made me nauseous.

"*You* talk about it!" I shouted. I jumped to my feet. I pushed my mother out of the way, dodged past Julie, who uttered a startled cry, and bolted to the front door.

I leaped out onto the front stoop and slammed the door hard behind me, shutting out their cries and pleas to come back. I took a deep breath of the fresh, warm spring air, dove off the stoop, and started to run.

I hesitated, seeing my car at the curb. No. I needed to run. I needed to run off my anger. I needed to feel the air against my face and let the silence clear my mind.

I lowered my head and picked up speed, my bag bouncing on my shoulder, swinging my arms as I ran through the night. Past mostly dark houses and small front yards, an empty lot with a FOR SALE sign near the curb, a narrow playground with a swing set and slide.

They think I'm crazy.

Julie thinks I'm crazy.

Some friend.

I knew this would happen if I confided in someone. And now here I was, running full speed, running like an animal at night, running who knows where. On my own.

Deena Fear couldn't help. Julie couldn't help. God knows, my parents couldn't help. They looked ready to have me locked up.

So here I was running along the street, running two blocks, then three, in and out of the dim spotlights of yellow light from the streetlights. Light, then shadow.

Would the rest of my life be spent in shadow?

I couldn't run forever. Even in my crazed state, I knew I'd have to go home. And then what?

My shoes pounded the soft grass. Somewhere in the distance a car horn honked three short beeps. The only other sound was the thudding of my shoes on the dew-wet ground.

When I neared the bus shelter on the corner, I stumbled to a stop. Had to catch my balance. My breaths came so hard, my chest ached.

I caught myself, my arms flailing, the bag suddenly heavy on my shoulder. Stopped, struggling to breathe, and stared at the glass bus shelter, lighted by a tall streetlight.

Stared at the stain of bright red through the glass. Squinted hard, focusing . . . until I saw that the blotch of red was a red hoodie. Through the shelter glass, I saw the red hoodie. And the boy wearing it. Hood pulled over his head. The boy hunched on the edge of the shelter bench, tapping one leg up and down.

Blade. He didn't see me. His back was turned, as if he was watching for the bus. But I knew. I knew he was waiting for me.

How did he know I would be here? It didn't matter. He was haunting me. I knew he would show up everywhere I went. I knew he would always be there.

I watched him, tapping his foot so casually, rubbing the knees of his jeans. I stood there, fists clenched, letting my anger grow until I saw red spots before my eyes, as red as his hoodie. And now I was seething, boiling over, swept up in a tidal wave of fury.

He can't do this to me!

Deena Fear's words came back to me then. I could hear her as if she were standing beside me. *"You have to kill him again."*

And I already had the knife from my bag. Already had the handle gripped tightly in my fist. The blade still blood-smeared from before.

I had never cleaned it. I had never tossed it away or hid it. I kept it . . . kept it because maybe I knew all along that I would have to use it again.

I wanted to shout. I wanted to scream out my fury. But

I held it in. I held it in, not breathing, no longer thinking like a human. I held it all in and raised the knife in front of me.

I slipped into the bus shelter before he could turn around—and I stabbed him in the back. Sank the blade into the middle of the red hoodie, sank it deep and pushed, pushed it deeper, pushed it with all my anger.

I slashed it to the right. Then pulled back and sliced it to the left. Dug it in and stabbed and sliced.

His arms flew up weakly. He uttered a long low groan of pain. Then sank forward. Just collapsed on himself.

Panting like a dog, wheezing loudly, I raised my eyes— and started to choke. I started to gag and choke because I saw Blade watching me. Blade, in his red hoodie, watching me from under a streetlight across the street.

39.

The knife fell from my hand and bounced into the curb. A cold grin spread over Blade's face, and he flashed me a thumbs-up.

A low howl escaped my throat. My knees started to fold. I grabbed the back of the shelter bench to keep myself up.

I sucked in a deep breath and held it. Then I reached over the back of the bench and grabbed the boy in front of me by the shoulders of his hoodie. I turned him around.

The hood fell back and I saw his lifeless face. Wide dark eyes staring blankly up at me. Mouth frozen open in a startled cry of pain. Curly brown hair matted to his forehead. A silver ring in one ear.

I've never seen him before.

Oh my God. Oh my God. I killed a stranger. I killed the wrong boy.

Over the throbbing pulses of blood at my temples, I

heard Blade's laughter. High, giddy laughter, as if he had just heard a funny joke.

I gazed across the street. But he had vanished into the deep shadows. His laughter faded slowly.

I realized I was still gripping the dead boy's shoulders. I had the sudden impulse to pull him to his feet. To tell him he was okay. To make him walk away.

His head fell back, smacking the bench loudly. The sound sent a shattering chill down my body. I let go of his shoulders. I stumbled back.

I'm a murderer.

"Deena! Did you make me do this?" I shouted, surprising myself. "Did you make me kill this boy, too?"

Silence.

Of course I heard only silence.

Deena was nowhere near.

I killed this one. I killed this boy. Not Deena.

I jumped as pale light spread over the grass. I turned to see a light go on in the front window of the house on the corner. Squinting up the lawn, I could see two people staring out the window at me.

I'm a murderer. I'm going to be caught.

I moved to the curb. I bent and picked up the knife. My hands trembled as I folded it and let it drop back into my bag.

Blade's cold laughter rang in my ears. I couldn't see him. But I could hear his gleeful, scornful laugh.

Covering my ears with both hands, I took off running again.

Running across the street and along the curb of the next block. Running. Holding my ears, shutting out the cold laughter of a dead boy.

Running into a blur of gray and purple and black night. Running. But, where?

I thought of Miranda. My only other friend. No. No way. Miranda wouldn't believe me, either. Why should she? I was sure Julie had already been on the phone with her, already shared what I had confided, already described the meeting with my parents. The ambush.

I was sure they had already discussed my *breakdown*. Crazy Caitlyn and her delusions of her dead boyfriend returning to haunt her. I was sure my two friends were very sympathetic. They wished there was something . . . anything . . . they could do to help me recover my sanity.

Yikes.

I couldn't run to Miranda's house. No way. Miranda wouldn't help me.

So where could I go? Where could I go with a blood-stained knife in my bag and chilling laughter in my ears? And the picture of me stabbing that boy, slashing and slicing him, stabbing him again and again, a stranger . . . the picture lingering in my eyes, replaying itself with every footstep.

Where could I go?

I had no choice. I had to go home. I had to surrender, to give up, to turn myself in, to confess my guilt, to prepare to face the consequences and pay for what I did.

Okay. Maybe I wasn't thinking clearly, Diary. Maybe my thoughts were a jumble. But that's what I was thinking as I ran down the dark, empty streets.

Back to Julie's house. My car parked at the curb. All the lights off in her house. The car bathed in darkness.

I fumbled for the key. Drove home in a frenzied blur of lights and passing houses and trees. Drove home without stopping, without seeing stop signs or traffic lights.

And when my house came into view, the world finally came back into focus. I actually felt relieved. I could stop running. Maybe I could find some safety inside.

My parents would be horrified when I confessed everything to them. They wouldn't understand. And it would be hard to make them believe me. But they would try to help me. I knew I could count on that.

My shoes slipped on the wet grass as I started to the kitchen door. I stopped short when a figure jumped out from the darkness at the side of the house.

Blade. Eyes glowing. He grabbed my arm with his remaining hand. "Time for you to join me, Caitlyn," he rasped through his ragged, torn lips.

I tried to tug free, but he was too strong. He pulled me toward him. Slipped a hand behind my head. And forced his lips against mine. His cold, dead lips, grinding against mine.

My stomach churned. I couldn't end the kiss. His mouth scraped against mine. I could feel the bump of stitches that he had missed.

Sick. I'm going to be sick.

The horrifying kiss seemed to last forever. Finally, Blade pulled his head back. He stared into my eyes. His glowing green eyes had no pupils. They were solid glass.

"It's time, Caitlyn," he repeated. "Time for you to come with me."

I gasped. "Come? Come where?"

He slid his face close to my ear and whispered: "*To the grave.*"

40.

"**N**ooooo!"

The scream burst from deep in my chest.

"Nooooo!" I tossed my head back and shrieked. Gathering all my strength, I shot my arms out and broke his hold on me.

He stumbled back. I struggled to breathe, the cold, sour taste of his lips still on mine.

With a desperate cry, I spun away and searched the ground for my bag. It had fallen into a flower bed at the side of the driveway. I took a step toward it, and Blade came at me. Arms outstretched, he roared as he prepared to tackle me.

I swung to the right and wriggled out of his reach as he dove. He shot past me and plunged to the ground, uttering a cry of surprise.

I made a grab for the bag. But he wrapped a hand around it before I could get there. He tossed it in the air. I watched it come down on the roof of my car.

As he climbed to his feet, grunting and growling like an angry animal, I raced to the car. I pulled the bag off the roof, gripping the handle in both hands.

Blade slashed a fist at me. I ducked, and the punch sailed over my head.

"You're coming with me," he growled. "You're dead, too, Caitlyn. You and I, we're dead together."

"No way!" I cried. I shot my hand into the bag, frantically pushing everything out of the way, fumbling, as I watched him prepare to lunge at me again.

There!

I had it. The knife at the bottom of the bag. The knife that had already killed him once. I wrapped my trembling fingers around the handle.

As he dove for me, I slid the blade out and swiped the knife at him.

Missed.

He slammed into the car, so hard it shook on its tires. He uttered a muffled gasp. Bounced off.

I spun and tried to drive the blade into his back.

"*Kill him again.*" Those were Deena's instructions. That was her only solution. The only way to get rid of a dead boyfriend. "*Kill him again.*"

He twisted his body to the side. The knife blade cut only air.

Green eyes glowing angrily, he raised both hands toward me.

I swung the knife again, off-balance this time. He

lurched forward and grabbed my arm. Grabbed my hand and struggled to pull the knife free.

I opened my mouth to protest, but I was breathing too hard, wheezing noisily. No sound escaped my mouth.

I tried to pull my arms away, to twist my body away from him. But he wrapped his hand around mine. And grabbed the knife from me.

A wide-eyed look of triumph spread for only an instant over his dead, pale face. And then he moved toward me, holding the knife blade high, aimed at my heart. He swung it down fast.

I stumbled and fell. Fell flat on my back. And before I could scramble to my feet, Blade was on top of me. He straddled my body, his knees digging into my sides.

I shoved him with both hands. Desperate to squirm out from under him. But he had me pinned down. Helpless.

The blank eyes bulging in his head, he raised the knife high, and I watched the blade, the gleaming blade, come plunging down.

41.

A scream escaped my throat. With a burst of strength, I grabbed his hand before he could bury the knife in me. Straining, groaning, I pushed the hand away.

We fought, a desperate wrestling match, me on my back, Blade straddling me, bent over me, using all his strength against me to push the blade down.

I gasped as the blade point came within an inch of my neck. With a superhuman heave, I shoved it back up. Blade uttered a cry of anger, frustrated that he could not stab me.

I twisted my body, struggling to squirm out from under him. Twisted hard—and saw Deena Fear running up the driveway.

"Deena—" I gasped her name.

Blade raised his head, turned to the driveway. He stopped his attempts to force the blade down. Just for a second, he loosened up.

And I took advantage to swipe the knife from his hand.

He was still gazing at Deena as I steadied the knife,

raised the blade, and plunged it up, straight up, into his stomach.

He uttered a breathy gasp. His hands flew up.

I stabbed him again. Stabbed the top of his stomach. Sliced through the red hoodie. Cut and sliced. Stabbed his chest between his ribs. Again. Again.

No blood this time. How could there be blood? He was dead. And now he was dead again, only he didn't seem to realize it.

I couldn't see Deena's face. Her hair blew wild about her head, covering her face. She stood with her arms crossed at the edge of the driveway, stood very still, made no attempt to interfere. As if she wasn't surprised. As if this was what she expected to find.

Finally, Blade uttered a final groan. His body started to slump to the right. I reached up, grabbed his side, and gave a hard push. He fell off me, his head bouncing on the grass.

I slid away from him. Gave him another push. He was stretched out on his side on the ground now. Eyes wide open but not moving. Not moving. Still as death.

Deena rushed forward and helped pull me to my feet. I stood there, my face wet with tears, my arms aching from the battle, blood pulsing at my temples.

My knees buckled and I started to fall. Deena held onto me, kept me standing up. I leaned against her. I couldn't catch my breath. I felt like I was choking.

"Wh-what are we going to do?" I stammered, my voice a choked rasp.

"Easy. Take it easy," Deena said softly, holding onto me. "I'll take care of it."

I blinked. Wiped the cold sweat off my forehead with the back of my hand. "Take care of it? How do you mean?"

She didn't answer. I started to feel a little more normal. My arms ached from my struggle with Blade. My neck felt stiff and sore. I glimpsed Blade, sprawled lifelessly on his side, head tilted at a strange angle, mouth hanging open.

"What do you mean take care of it?" I repeated.

Deena tugged her wild hair off her face with both hands. "I'll take him back to the chapel. Return him to his coffin."

I studied her eyes, trying to determine if she was telling the truth. Did she mean it? Would she leave him dead this time? Not bring him back to torture me some more? Not bring him back in hopes that he would be *hers* next time?

"His family will want to bury him right away," Deena murmured. She motioned to the body. "Help me get him in my car."

I started to follow her across the grass. "I'll come with you," I said. "I want to make sure—"

"No. You're totally messed up," Deena said. "He nearly killed you, Caitlyn. Go inside. Take a long hot bath. Get some rest."

"But I should—" I tried to protest.

She waved me back. "No. Just help me lift him into my backseat. I can do this myself. Really." I grabbed his legs. She started to lift him from under the shoulders. "It's my fault, after all," she said. "I never should have brought him back. I . . . I'm sorry."

I didn't reply to that. I felt too weary. I could barely hold my head up. Blade weighed more than I thought. Or maybe it's just that dead bodies are really heavy.

We dragged him to her car at the bottom of the driveway. We lifted him off the ground and heaved him face-down onto the backseat. His legs stuck stiffly out of the car. Deena carefully tucked him in and slammed the door.

She walked to the driver's door. "I can handle this. Seriously," she said. "Go inside, Caitlyn. Get some rest."

I won't be able to rest. How can I rest after what I did tonight?

I stared into her headlights as she backed down the drive. My mind was spinning. My whole body ached. I decided I had to follow her.

She had aroused my suspicions. Why did she insist on returning Blade to the chapel on her own. I didn't think she was just being considerate of me. I didn't think she was that worried about me.

What did she really plan to do? Was she telling the truth, or did she have another plan for Blade's body?

The lights were on in the den at the far side of my house. I knew my parents were waiting there. I slipped into the car and, as silently, as I could, backed slowly down the driveway with the headlights off.

I could see Deena's car a block or so ahead of me. I kept the lights off. I didn't want her to see me following. I slowed down as she stopped for a light. She made a right turn and I waited, even though the light was green.

There was no traffic on the road, so I let her get a three-block lead. Was this the way to the chapel? I'd been concentrating so hard on the back of her car that I hadn't looked to see where we were.

Deena's twin red brake lights floated in front of my eyes. I saw her make another right turn. I kept thinking about Blade, back in his coffin. Blade finally buried deep in the ground where he couldn't come after me, where he couldn't try to pull me with him.

I was nearly to the right turn when I heard the rise and fall of the siren and saw the flashing lights in my rearview mirror.

As the patrol car came into focus in the mirror, I let out a groan and swung the car to the right. The cop car edged past me, and I saw a dark-uniformed officer in the passenger seat wave me to the curb.

I hope Deena really is returning Blade's body to the chapel.

That was my first thought. My second thought was more frightening: *Are the police stopping me because they know I killed Blade? Have they finally solved the case? Are they arresting me for murder?*

I gripped the wheel with both hands and clenched my jaw, trying to stop the chills that ran down my body.

I stared straight ahead until I heard the hard tap on my window. I turned and saw Officer Rivera peering in at me. "Caitlyn? Is that you? Step out of the car, please."

42.

I grabbed the door handle, then hesitated. I spun around and saw my bag on the seat. Was the knife inside it? Or had I left it on the ground near my driveway where it had fallen?

Rivera tapped impatiently on the window. "Please step out of the car." He raised a flashlight and sent a white beam of halogen light over my face.

I shut my eyes and climbed out of the car. I stood there stiffly, blinking in the bright light. "Wh-what's wrong?" I stammered softly. I tensed myself for the bad news.

I turned away from the light and glimpsed his partner still behind the wheel of the patrol car. Rivera studied me intently. He had one hand on his holster.

Ready to arrest me for murder.

He lowered the light from my face. "Caitlyn, were you aware that you were driving without headlights?"

"Huh? Excuse me?"

"Didn't you notice your headlights were off? Didn't it seem a little dark to you?"

"Well . . ." My throat tightened. I couldn't speak. I wanted to burst out laughing. I was expecting to be hand-cuffed and dragged off to prison for murder. And these guys pulled me over because of my headlights.

I pressed my hand over my mouth so he wouldn't see my grin.

"Caitlyn, have you been drinking?" Rivera brought his face close to mine, I guess, to smell my breath.

"I don't drink," I said.

"It's pretty late," he said, his eyes glancing around the dark street. "Where are you going this time of night?"

"I'm just . . . coming from a friend's house," I said. "My friend Julie."

"And where does Julie live?"

"On Bank Street. A couple of blocks from the mall."

He nodded. He took off his cap and swept back his black hair. "Well, I'll let you go," he said. "Is everything okay? Did you just forget about the headlights?"

I nodded. "Yeah. I was thinking about school. I just forgot."

He pushed down his cap. "Well, be careful, okay? Put on your lights."

"Will do," I said. I watched him walk back to the patrol car. He slid into the passenger seat and closed the door. He and his partner didn't pull out. I guess they were waiting for me to go first.

I clicked on the headlights. Then I shifted into drive and drove away. Too late to try to catch up with Deena. I turned at the next block and made my way toward home.

A heavy wave of dread rolled over me. My stomach began to ache. I knew my parents were waiting up for me. How would I explain tonight to them? What was I going to say?

I'm sure they were mortified to have that emotional confrontation with me in front of Julie's parents. And how could I explain it? As I pulled up the driveway, my brain was doing jumping jacks in my head, leaping from thought to thought until I felt like my head was about to blow apart.

Sure enough, the front door swung open before I even climbed out of the car, and Mom and Dad came rushing at me. "Are you okay? Where did you go? How do you feel?"

I had the car door open only a few inches. "At least, let me out of the car," I said.

They obediently stepped back. I climbed out, straightening my top over my jeans. They put their arms around my shoulders and we walked into the house in a line.

"Can you explain to me what's going on?" Dad demanded after we had settled on facing couches in the den.

"I'm perfectly fine," I said. "I'm just tired, that's all. Way tired. But I'm okay. Seriously." *Especially since Blade is dead again and won't be coming to haunt me.*

"Do you expect us to believe that?" Mom said, arms

crossed tightly in front of her. She's the tough one. I knew I'd have trouble getting past her.

"Well . . . yes," I said. "I do expect you to believe me. I'm not a liar, Mom. I think you know that."

She ignored that. "Where did you go?" she demanded, eyes piercing mine. I could practically feel the heat from them. "Where did you go after you ran out of Julie's?"

I shrugged. "Just drove around."

"Caitlyn, you have to explain what's going on," Dad said, his fingers tapping the couch arm. "What did you tell Julie? What did you say to get your friend so upset?"

"You have to tell us," Mom insisted. "You can't just shrug it off and not say anything."

"Look, it was a joke," I said. "I made up a story about Blade Hampton and—"

"That boy who died?" Mom interrupted. She shook her head. "That was so sad."

"Yes, Blade Hampton," I said. I shut my eyes and rubbed my temples. "It was a joke. I told Julie a story about him and . . . I forgot she doesn't have a sense of humor. I guess she thought I was serious."

They both stared at me in silence. Were they buying my lame story?

No. Not at all.

Too late to make up a new one.

A hush fell over the room. Dad tapped the couch arm rhythmically. Mom didn't move. She finally broke the silence. "Well, Caitlyn . . . your joke must not have been too funny. Whatever you said to her got her so upset, she called us and said you were having a breakdown."

I forced a laugh. "Breakdown? What's a breakdown? You mean like a car?"

"Don't be glib," Dad said sharply. "Your friend was really upset and worried about you."

"Sorry," I muttered. "But you've got to believe me. It was all a joke. I guess Julie took it the wrong way. I'm perfectly okay. I'm not a wacko. I haven't gone berserk or anything."

I started to stand up. Maybe I could make it to the stairs and escape to my room. I could see from their faces that they were unsatisfied.

My parents aren't dumb. In fact, they're really smart. And they knew they weren't getting a very good explanation from me. They knew they weren't getting any explanation at all.

"You'd better go to bed," Dad said, motioning to the stairs. His expression was suddenly sad, his eyes weary, as if I had disappointed him.

"But we're not finished," Mom said, jumping up and leaning over me. "We're not finished, Caitlyn. We'll come back to this, hear me. We'll talk when you're not so exhausted."

"Good," I said. I didn't know what else to say. I stopped at the den doorway and turned back to them. "Sorry," I murmured. "Sorry you got that phone call from Julie and had to run over there. Sorry. Seriously. Sorry if you were

worried about me . . ." My voice trailed off. "Goodnight."
I grabbed the banister and pulled myself up the stairs.

I paused at the top of the stairs. I could still hear Mom and Dad, both talking heatedly in the den. I heard Dad say, "Teenagers all have secrets. But she'll be okay."

Secrets? He didn't know the half of it.

I picked up a stray sock that someone must have dropped in the hall and carried it to my room. I closed the bedroom door carefully behind me. The window was closed and the air was stuffy, but I didn't bother to open it. I began to pace tensely back and forth. My room is small. Not much room to pace. I felt like a caged animal.

How would I ever get to sleep?

If Blade was safely back in his coffin, maybe I could begin to rest again. I'd be in even better shape if I knew his coffin was deep in the ground.

But I had no way of knowing Deena's real intentions. I didn't trust her. I knew she was insane about Blade. But . . . insane enough to awake him again? To try her magic on him one more time?

"No. No way," I muttered to myself.

I had no way to get in touch with her. She wasn't responding to texts or phone calls. It was too late to sneak out and drive to her house. I just had to pray that she returned Blade's body as she said she would.

I changed into a nightshirt, clicked off the light, and climbed into bed. My hands felt clammy. My heart was still racing. My mind skipped from thought to thought, from ugly picture to ugly picture.

I killed someone. I killed someone tonight. . . .

I knew it would take a long time to fall asleep, Diary, and it did. I lay staring at the shadows on the window for at least an hour. Somehow, I finally felt myself fading into unconsciousness.

I fell into a deep, dreamless sleep. I must have slept a long time.

When I opened my eyes, red morning sunlight filled the window and poured onto the foot of my bed. I blinked, and slowly realized I'd been awakened by a sound. I started to pull myself up, listening hard.

Yes. A tapping sound. *Tap tap tap.* Soft but insistent.

Tapping on the window. I raised my eyes. A shadow appeared in the red sunlight.

I held my breath. Terror made me grip the bed sheet with both hands.

Tap tap tap.

Someone tapping on my bedroom window. Just inches away from me.

Blade!

43.

The tapping repeated, but the shadow vanished from the window glass. I forced myself to sit up.

Oh, please, no. Go away, Blade. Please go away.

Another drumbeat of soft taps.

Shielding my eyes from the bright sun with one hand, I peered out.

"Blade?"

I uttered a long sigh of relief.

Not Blade.

A woodpecker perched on the siding beside the window, pecked away, tapping its steady rhythm.

If I was in a normal state of mind, I would have remembered. This wasn't the first morning that woodpecker decided to have breakfast right outside my room.

But I wasn't in a normal state of mind. And as I got dressed for school, I wondered sadly if I'd *ever* be in a normal state again.

★   ★   ★

I avoided Julie and Miranda at school. I saw them watching me from across the hall before homeroom. They were whispering, their faces close together, peering at me as if I were crazy or some strange new animal species.

Julie started toward me. Maybe she wanted to apologize again for getting my parents on my case. But I wasn't ready to tell her everything was hunky-dory again. I felt betrayed. I knew I'd probably get over that. But not yet.

I slammed my locker door and hurried off in the other direction, leaving them both open-mouthed behind me. I stepped into the classroom and searched up and down for Blade. Can you blame me?

He'd surprised me in school before, the day I tried to read my violin essay. I had no guarantee he wouldn't be back to haunt me. No guarantee he wouldn't be waiting for me, waiting to grab me in English class, or my Advanced Math class, or in the library where I had my fourth-period study hall.

I knew I had to stay alert all day, Diary. It wasn't easy. It was a horrible way to spend the day, always frightened, never able to relax or let my guard down for a second.

At lunch period, I grabbed a tuna fish sandwich in the lunchroom and carried it outside to the parking lot. I didn't want to run into Julie and Miranda. We always sat together at a table on the far side, and I figured it would be less awkward for all three of us if I ate outside by myself.

It was a warm day, with strong sunlight making it feel

more like summer than spring. The daffodils behind the school, bright as sunshine, fluttered in a soft breeze. Two squirrels scampered together along the edge of the parking lot.

I leaned against the trunk of my car and tried to eat the sandwich. But my throat was dry and I didn't bring anything to drink. I wasn't hungry anyway. My stomach was knotted tight.

Suddenly, I knew what I had to do. The rest of the school day would be a nightmare if I continued to expect seeing Blade. I couldn't go back inside.

I climbed into my car and tossed the uneaten sandwich on the passenger seat. I fumbled the key from my bag and started the engine.

The North Hills Chapel was a short drive from school. My plan was to drive to the chapel and make sure that Blade had been returned. Once I knew that for sure, I could return to school and maybe . . . just maybe . . . my life would start to return to normal.

When I arrived at the chapel, I found the front doors open. Blue-uniformed workers were setting up ladders on one wall, preparing to clean the stained glass windows that ran along the ceiling.

I started to the front, searching for someone who could help me. And nearly got tangled in a wide canvas tarp two men were spreading over the aisle.

"Is anyone here?" My voice came out louder than I'd planned. Several of the workers turned to look at me.

A gray-haired woman in a maid's uniform had been hidden behind the podium on the altar. She poked her head up, a dust cloth in her hand. "Can I help you?"

I nodded. "Yes. I'm trying to get some information."

Before she could answer, the minister appeared from the back hall. Reverend Preller was wearing the same brown sport jacket he had worn at Blade's funeral. He carried a clipboard in one hand and had a pen tucked behind one ear.

He narrowed his eyes at me. "Yes?"

A crash behind me made me jump. I turned to see that one of the workers had dropped a bucket. The soapy water flowed over the carpeted aisle.

The minister scratched the back of his hair. "As you can see, we're closed today. But if you need information—?"

I suddenly realized I didn't know how to ask my question. I couldn't just blurt out "Is Blade Hampton in his coffin?" I stood there with my mouth hanging open, thinking hard.

"I . . . I came to ask about Blade Hampton," I finally managed to say.

His eyes flashed. His features tightened. I'd definitely grabbed his attention.

"The funeral was last Saturday. Are you a relative?" he asked, studying me intently.

"Yes," I lied. "He . . . he was my cousin." My heart began to thud. Did he believe me?

"Well, I can't really tell you—" he started.

"I just need to know where he's buried," I said. "I . . . My family got to Shadyside late. And we need to know . . ."

He scratched the back of his hair again. "Buried?"

I nodded, biting my bottom lip.

Please answer. Please tell me that he has been buried.

"Miss, have you talked to Blade's parents? If so, you know they are in shock. You know they are beyond themselves with grief."

"W–We . . . we just got here," I stammered. "We haven't had a chance—"

"Blade hasn't been buried," Preller said. "Because his body has been stolen."

44.

"Oh, wow." I couldn't hide my horror and disappointment. I could feel the blood rushing to my face. My knees started to fold. Deena didn't return him to his coffin.

I don't know what Reverend Preller thought. I really didn't care. Blade was out there somewhere. And I knew he wouldn't rest till he dragged me with him, dragged me to my death.

"Sorry for the shock," he said. But I had already spun away from him and was running full speed, running past the startled workers.

To my car. I slammed the door. Started it up. Pounded my foot on the gas until the engine roared. I wanted to roar along with it. I wanted to roar and scream and howl like a wild animal.

I don't want to die, Blade. I don't want to join you.

But I knew he was waiting somewhere for me. Deena Fear was a liar. Not just a liar, she was evil. She couldn't give up her desperate hope that Blade would decide he wanted her instead of me.

She couldn't give up. . . .

I pounded the steering wheel with both fists. Pounded till both hands ached. One of the chapel workers stopped to peer in at me. I turned my head away, and he kept walking.

I didn't know if I was more frightened or angry. I only knew I was about to go insane, totally berserk.

It was time to tell my parents. I had no choice. It was time to tell them the whole story. I knew it would be impossible for them to believe what had happened in the last few weeks.

But I had to try. . . .

I knew they were both home. Mom thought she might be coming down with the flu, and Dad took a personal day so he could stay home and take care of her.

I burst into the house, my head spinning. *Where do I start? How do I start to tell them what has happened?*

I didn't want to burst into tears and be unable to talk. But as I ran through the house, I wasn't sure I could hold myself together.

"Mom? Dad?" I found them sitting side by side on the couch in the den. I roared into the room. Opened my mouth to try to start my story. Stopped when I saw what they had on their laps.

And let out a horrified scream: "What are you *doing* with that?"

45.

I stood there, my finger trembling as I pointed at my diary. My diary sitting open in front of them.

"How did you get that? What are you doing with that?" I screamed.

Dad went pale. Mom was the first to speak. "Cathy-Ann, I know we shouldn't have read it. I know we invaded your privacy. But it was open on your desk and . . . and . . ."

"We were so worried about you." Dad finished her sentence.

"B-B-But—" I sputtered.

"We had to find out what has been troubling you," Mom said. "Cathy-Ann, we had no idea. Reading your diary . . . So much violence. And killing. And crazy things happening."

"Your diary reads like a horror story," Dad said. His eyes were wet. His chin trembled. He was as pale as the sofa cushion.

"It *is* a horror story!" I cried, rushing over to them, standing above them."

"Why did you change your name?" Mom demanded. "Why did you call yourself Caitlyn?"

I let out a long sigh. "Because it's just a story, Mom. It isn't my diary. It isn't a diary at all."

Mom blinked. "But Cathy-Ann . . . all your friends are in it. Julie and Miranda. They're real people. And your teachers are in it. And—"

"I used them in my story, Mom. I used them as characters because I knew them. I knew how to describe them. But it isn't true. It's not a diary. It's a novel I've been writing. None of it is true. I swear. None of it."

Dad swallowed hard. He kept blinking, as if he was having trouble focusing. "It's a novel? It's fiction?"

"Yes, I've been writing a novel," I said. I rolled my eyes. I let out a bitter laugh. "Did you two honestly believe that I killed a boy? Seriously? You believed I stabbed a boy to death—*twice*? Did you?"

Mom hesitated. "Well . . . no. Of course not, dear. But that boy Blade *did* die. He drowned, didn't he? On vacation with his parents?"

I nodded. "It was very upsetting. He was a friend of mine. So I used him in the story. But—"

"It says you killed a stranger," Mom said, biting her bottom lip. "You wrote that you stabbed an innocent boy in a bus shelter. Cathy-Ann—?"

"It isn't true. It's all made up," I insisted. "It's fiction, Mom. Can't you understand?"

"Well, who is this Deena Fear?" Dad demanded. "I never heard you mention her before."

I rolled my eyes again. "That's because she doesn't exist, Dad. There *is* no Deena Fear. I made her up. You know all those crazy stories people tell about Fear Street. I made up a new one."

He nodded, exchanging a glance with Mom. She ran her hand over a handwritten page in her lap. "Well, Cathy-Ann, this is quite a piece of writing. But . . . I'm sorry to say this, but it's the work of a very troubled person."

"Maybe you need to see someone," Dad said. "These thoughts you have here—"

"You two are ridiculous," I said. "I'm not troubled at all. You know I love to write. I decided to write a horror novel. That's all. I used my imagination. I dreamed up a frightening story."

I tugged at both sides of my hair. "But that doesn't mean I'm troubled. That doesn't mean I have horrifying abnormal thoughts. I made up characters and I wrote a story. Can't you two understand that?"

They shook their heads. They couldn't get over the fact that my writing was filled with violence and blood and murder and a boy coming back from the dead. I guess they thought I should write about kittens and lollipops.

I reached out both hands and Mom handed me the book. "You should be proud of me," I said. "Look how creative I am. I do my schoolwork. I have a B-plus average. And I've written almost an entire novel."

I shook my head, frowning at them. "Instead of sitting there with those disapproving expressions on your faces, you should be telling me what a cool thing I've done."

I turned and started from the den. But Dad called me back. "You're right. You're totally right," he said. "We *are* proud of you, Cathy-Ann. We just didn't understand. . . ." He shook his head. "You took us by surprise. You completely fooled us. The writing is so good, we believed it all."

"Your dad is right," Mom said. She pointed to the book in my hands. "You know what? It really is a good story. Maybe you should try to get it published.

ONE YEAR LATER

46.

Cathy-Ann straightened her skirt over her tights, then swept back her hair with both hands. She shielded her eyes from the bright afternoon sunlight and peered across the parking lot to the bookstore.

"Look, dear, there's already a line," her mother said. "Isn't it exciting? They're waiting for *you*."

Exciting isn't the word, Cathy-Ann thought, feeling her heart begin to flutter in her chest. *It's unreal!*

Her dad took her arm and she walked between her parents toward the bookstore. She counted at least twenty people lined up outside the entrance. Most of them were high school girls. She recognized a few from Shadyside High. But she saw a sprinkling of adults there, too.

She stopped in front of the big window at the side of the entrance and peered through the sun glare at the poster—her photo, smiling and holding the book. Below it, the words in bold type: **APPEARING TODAY. SIGNING AT** 3:00.

Dad pulled out his phone and snapped a few photos of the display. A few people in the line recognized her and called out to her.

The door opened. A pleasant-looking young woman in jeans and a red-and-white striped t-shirt stepped out to greet her. "Hi, Cathy-Ann. I'm Mandy Wade, the store manager. Welcome to Books & Things."

"Thank you." Cathy-Ann felt her throat tighten. *Was this really happening?*

What a crazy year it had been. It had taken weeks to type up what she had written in the diary. Then she sent the manuscript to her cousin Barry in New York, whose girlfriend worked in publishing. What a shock when, two weeks later, Cathy-Ann received an offer for the book. It was going to be published!

Now here she was, about to do her very first book-signing at the only bookstore in Shadyside. The book had been out for only a week and had already received some good reviews.

Cathy-Ann had to laugh. Here was Mom beaming proudly as they walked through the bookstore. She had been so appalled and upset the first time she read the story. Now she kept a Pinterest page of photos and reviews and everything about the book.

"Sit behind the table here," Mandy Wade said, pulling out the chair for Cathy-Ann. "I have a lot of different pens and markers. I didn't know which you prefer."

"I don't really know, either," Cathy-Ann replied, sitting down next to the tall stack of her books. This is my first signing."

Mandy patted her hand. "The main thing is to relax and enjoy it. These people came all the way here to see you. So there's no reason to be nervous." She turned to the front. "I'm going to let people in now. You have a great crowd for a first-time author."

Cathy-Ann's dad was busy taking photos of her. Her mom stood at the side, arms crossed, a proud grin stuck on her face.

Cathy-Ann cleared her throat, opened the water bottle in front of her, and took a long sip. Then she picked up a pen and watched as people began to stream toward the table.

The first two in line were Rachel Martin and Amy O'Brien, two girls from her senior class at Shadyside High. They chatted about how exciting this was. "I've already read it," Amy said as Cathy-Ann thanked her and signed their books.

A middle-aged woman set a book down in front of Cathy-Ann and opened it to the title page. "Could you sign this to my daughter Coral? She likes to write, too. Could you write something encouraging to her?"

Cathy-Ann signed the book to Coral. She didn't really know what to say, so she wrote: "Keep reading and keep writing!"

The next woman had bought three books she wanted signed. "No message. Just sign your name. They're going to be birthday gifts," she said.

Cathy-Ann leaned over the books and signed them. "Are you working on another book?" the woman asked, gathering them up.

"Not yet," Cathy-Ann said.

Next in line was a tall young man with wavy black hair and silvery sunglasses that caught the light from the ceiling. He set a book down in front of her. Then he slowly removed the sunglasses.

She stared into his strange gray-green eyes—and recognized him.

He shoved the book toward her. "Just sign it to The Dead Boyfriend," he said.

"Blade? Blade?"

Cathy-Ann dropped her pen and started to scream.